A DRAGON CALLED
SHINING LEAVES

Books by Pam G Howard

The Ashridge Adventures

Prince of Dragons
King of Dragons

The McDragon Series

McDragon
Effel
McFinnia

Mr Spangle Series

Spangle

A DRAGON CALLED SHINING LEAVES

PAM G HOWARD

Matador
Unit E2 Airfield Business Park,
Harrison Road, Market Harborough,
Leicestershire. LE16 7UL
Tel: 0116 2792299
Email: books@troubador.co.uk
Web: www.troubador.co.uk/matador
Twitter: @matadorbooks

ISBN 978 1803133 249

British Library Cataloguing in Publication Data.
A catalogue record for this book is available from the British Library.

Printed and bound by CPI Group (UK) Ltd, Croydon, CR0 4YY
Typeset in 11pt Minion Pro by Troubador Publishing Ltd, Leicester, UK

Matador is an imprint of Troubador Publishing Ltd

For Caroline, with love.

CHAPTER ONE

TAN

Looking down at the jagged teeth of rocks below he realised he'd made a huge mistake. Had his foolishness brought him to his end? A big sigh hissed through his teeth as he clung onto the gritty grey rock in desperation, clenching his fingers to try and find a grip.

The whole reason for the stupidity of Tan making this ridiculous climb was because Otto had dared him to, and he wanted to try and heal the breach between them any way he could.

He looked up.

"Only halfway!" he puffed as his arms weakened and his fingers lost their hold – he was going to fall!

Air rushed past him as he plunged down and down – most certainly to find his death. As he fell, he let his thoughts go free to picture his mother with her greying hair and the determined look that she always had on her face, then his golden-haired sister, Roselda smiling happily as usual and finally, his fierce big brother, Leonard who was a soldier in the service of Lord Travers. Lastly, there was Autumn…

Suddenly his legs felt as if they were leaving their sockets, almost as if they'd been caught on a rock and his body shuddered to a halt.

"What the…!!"

Then he was moving again but rising!! He thrashed about as he screamed in fright trying to see what it was that had snatched him out of the air.

Long scaley huge legs ending in deep russet talons had a firm grip on him. Surely not?! This could be far worse than being splattered on the rocks below – he was going to be food for a monster!

Passing out, his last thoughts were thrust from his mind.

* * *

"Look at you! Did you reach the pinnacle? I didn't see you!" the voice jeered from the other side of the road.

"Drat!" thought Tan, "I thought I'd missed that brainless pig." He was feeling rather annoyed that his so-called best friend, Otto had issued the dangerous challenge of Tan climbing up to the mountain peak and he turned away to put off the meeting until he had calmed down.

"Not so fast!" and a meaty hand clamped tightly on his shoulder swinging his body around.

"What do you want Otto?"

"Just to look at the wimpy turd that you are, that's all!" was the sneering answer.

2

"What have I done to you to make you like this – we were friends, weren't we? Very good friends." Tan faced up to his opponent.

"That was before."

"Before what? I have no idea what's got into you! Now let me go, your father's librarian is expecting me, and you know he won't be happy if I'm late," he said grumpily looking up at the castle which was suspended in the rocky mountain above him.

Otto gave Tan a shove and stomped off whistling down the lane.

"What was that about," Tan muttered as he straightened his jacket before walking off in the direction of the track which led up to the Lord's castle. It was always a bit of a trek up to it, but worth it once he'd arrived.

He enjoyed the work he did in the library, particularly when he had to find old dusty tomes that hadn't seen the light of day for hundreds of years. They mentioned magic and wizards from years gone by. He always thought that the old librarian, Alton rather looked like a wizard might do, as opposed to someone who spent hours peering through his pince nez as he hunted for information that the books in the library contained. He was tall and slender with long straggly grey hair which the man was always trying to flatten and a beard which came down to his chest. He carried himself proudly yet when he spoke to his assistant it was in a surprisingly soft voice.

Opening the door to the library he stopped just inside and took a deep breath in – the smell of old parchment tickled his nose and made him sneeze as it did every single time, but he was still in awe of the huge number of

3

books which lined the circular panelled walls. There were thousands and thousands of them along with others which were piled up high on various tables scattered around the room. How Alton seemed to know what books were where was a total mystery to Tan.

"'There you are! At least I always know when you've arrived!" the librarian called over to him. "I need you to go into the archives as I am sure there is a map inside a book which gives details of the river and where it used to run years ago before it changed course. It is something that would be useful to know. Look for a grey cover."

Tan was about to say that nearly all of the books had grey covers when Alton added, "I think it is called Rivers of the Glades or something like that. Off you go now!"

The lad put his pack of sandwiches down on a nearby desk and set off in the direction of the archives. Motes of dust danced around in the stream of sunlight coming through the huge domed window above them.

The day passed in a flurry of activity and finally came to an end when the light began to fade making it impossible to see properly.

"Home time for you, young man," Alton called out as he rummaged around in one of his voluminous pockets fumbling for the long-stemmed pipe he kept there. He never lit it while in the library telling Tan that it was too much of a fire risk, which was the same reason they only used the lanterns hanging from wooden battens on the walls if there was something important that had to be found when it got dark.

CHAPTER TWO

AUTUMN

With her red hair streaming behind her Autumn urged her black pony, Blackberry, into a gallop, sheer joy making her whoop with delight. Freedom!

She'd spent the morning and part of the afternoon at the village school where her mother taught, and it was always a relief to get away. Some days could be slower than others because of the vast age range in the children attending. Autumn helped with the smaller children in an effort to give the older ones more chance to learn from her mother. She smiled when she thought of the time when she and Tan had been at school together, he was different from the other boys in that he had always grasped what they were being taught immediately, hence his being selected to work in the castle library.

When she reached the edge of the dark forest, she reluctantly turned Blackberry's head towards home. There were many tales of what lurked in the forest and she was not allowed to enter it.

They stopped a short way from home and weaved between some obstacles she'd set up there, practising leaning down and snatching up the various rocks with handles made of string tied around them which were randomly placed hither and thither. It was hard work but both Autumn and Blackberry enjoyed the concentration and effort it took. Still panting, she tugged her bow from her shoulders to aim an arrow at the target that was in a tree a good distance away.

"Perfect!" was all she could say as she watched it land dead centre.

After collecting the arrow they trotted back towards the smoke that was twisting up into the air from her father's forge, reminding herself how very lucky she was to have a pony of her own and be able to explore further afield than many others did.

"Oh no!" her heart sunk to her boots when she spotted Otto ambling along the lane leading to her home. It was too late to turn back.

"Hello!" he called out smiling.

A nod was all she could manage in return and although she slowed Blackberry to a walk, she pressed her calves firmly on his side to urge him to cross the ground quickly. The pony responded perfectly.

"Did you have a good ride?"

"Yes thanks," was the polite answer.

"Where did you go?"

It was always the same question from him even though he knew perfectly well that she wasn't allowed to go further than the outskirts of the forest.

Seeing him had quite spoiled some of the joy she'd had at getting away on her own and it was a relief when they reached the forge, pulling up just outside in the hope that the lad would take the hint and disappear.

There had been a time when she, Otto and Tan had been inseparable, spending as often as they could together, either in the castle or the fields surrounding the village but now a rift had appeared between the lads for some reason. When they were younger, a favourite game had been "Malvic will get you!" which even now, the younger children played. Malvic was supposed to be the devil who could eat you alive if he caught you. A strange game to be sure.

Her father was in the forge firmly gripping one of the hind legs of a huge cart horse – this particular horse always tried to rest its whole weight on the blacksmith while it was being shod and she was amazed that her father was strong enough to remain upright.

He elbowed it in the ribs shouting, "Get up you beasty!" and the animal shuffled its balance back onto the other three legs. He soon had the hoof shortened and rasped into a perfect shape.

Autumn hovered nearby watching, knowing that eventually Otto would sidle off because the heat belting out of the forge would get to him.

Her patience won in the end and as soon as he had disappeared around the corner she smiled at her dad and led the pony to his stall where she rubbed him down with a handful of straw to dry him off and then brushed him until his coat gleamed like midnight. Blackberry let her know he was enjoying the attention by nudging her and whickering with pleasure. Her next task was to muck out his stable and throw clean straw across the bed.

She was just admiring her handiwork when she heard Tan whistling as he traipsed down the winding road leading from the castle. He always seemed calm and content, rarely letting anything ruffle him.

He settled himself on a nearby bale of straw and chatted quietly as Autumn prepared Blackberry's feed.

An idea popped into her head when Tan mentioned the river that used to run near the village.

"Perhaps we could go out exploring one day like we used to and see if we can find the old riverbed?"

"That's a good plan, we haven't been out like that for a long while. When I'm in the library next I'll take another look at the map so we can get an idea of where to go."

"How about Sunday afternoon? I can make us up a picnic."

The lad beamed back at her.

"We might need to dodge Otto though because at the moment he seems to have an issue with me." Autumn raised her eyebrows as if in agreement.

"Tell you what, I'll ride Blackberry and meet you at the edge of the meadow – there's no way Otto can keep up with me if I'm on horseback."

CHAPTER THREE

TAN

Stretching contentedly in bed Tan thought about his brush with death. When he'd come around after his fall he'd found himself lying on a hard cold rocky floor in a cavern. It was a great relief to realise that there were no broken bones. But how on earth had he ended up here and not in pieces on the rocks below?

He'd looked about him rather surprised to spot a pile of rather musty acorns, quite a big pile in fact. Then he'd turned his head and sat bolt upright in shock!

"What the…!"

A big almond shaped eye stared back at him. It was at the end of a very long sinuous autumnal coloured neck. Surely not… could it be a dragon!?

"Don't eat me!"

There was a rumble and then a voice in his head answered him. "I wouldn't eat a scrawny thing like you!

You must be all bones and bits would stick in my teeth."
Was the dragon laughing at him?

"Why... why am I here? You saved me from crashing down on the rocks."

"Hmm, that I did. What were you doing climbing my rocks anyway?

"You probably wouldn't understand, it was a dare."

"Well... it is a strange thing to do when one is so thin and feeble looking."

Tan began to feel a little more confident that he wasn't going to be chewed up and spat out or burned to a crisp.

"How can it be that you, a dragon can speak to me? Am I really dead, is this just my brain having a last dance with life? I thought dragons were something that were just in fairy stories for children, rather like Malvic."

"You are very much alive, which is good because I have been wanting to speak to a human for some time."

The lad looked back at the dragon, "Well, I thank you from the bottom of my heart for saving me." He hesitated, "Can I ask, why is there a pile of acorns over there?"

"Bah... because I've found I have a liking for eating acorns, they make a tasty snack."

Puzzlement showed on Tan's face as he asked, "Why on earth can a dragon like eating acorns?" Followed swiftly by, "How am I going to get back down to the ground?"

* * *

It had been a huge relief to finally be back on terra-firma, the dragon having gathered him up in its taloned front paws and delivering him to the ground, leaving him with the instruction to return as soon as he could so they could talk some more. The dragon was fascinated by life in the village and had many questions and Tan in turn was eager to learn about dragons.

He found his sister at home helping his mother lay the table for dinner.

"You look as if you've been through a hedge backwards," his mum commented as she placed a bowl of delicious smelling stew down on the table.

"You could say that!" was his reply although he had no intention of letting her know what had really happened to him.

"Otto will be at the bottom of it," Roselda laughed.

His mother shot him a worried look, "What happened to your friendship with the boy? I thought you were best friends."

"So did I, but he won't tell me what has come between us."

"Well, it will not help Leonard's prospects if you fall out with the Lord's son." Leonard was his older brother.

"Don't worry mum, Leonard tells me that Lord Travers is a good and fair Lord. I have no idea what it is that has upset Otto, but I'm sure it will pass eventually."

His sister smirked, "Really!" but she didn't elucidate any further than that and Tan filled his mouth with food so that the subject could be dropped, table manners were important to his mum which meant he couldn't speak with his mouth full. Despite her young age, his sister always seemed to have the knack of knowing what other people were thinking.

The smell of the library enveloped Tan as he entered smiling happily.

"Some news for you, young man!" Alton waved him over.

"Yes, sir?"

"In a week's time you will accompany me to Lord Nivers' estate." Tan's eyes widened at the thought as he had never crossed beyond the boundary before – it was something that no-one from the village did unless they were a merchant selling their wares.

"Why are we doing that?" he asked eagerly.

"There could be trouble brewing further afield in the realm and Lord Travers has asked me to gather as much information as I can about it under the pretence of searching for some of the books in Lord Nivers' library. It's a trip that will take some weeks and you will need to make your mother aware of that. I shall give the shopkeeper coin to enable you to buy a cloak, some stout walking boots and good quality clothes so that you look the part of my apprentice when we arrive at our destination."

"So… we are to be spies?"

"Well, I suppose you could say that."

The rest of the day passed in a bit of a blur for Tan, but he did remember to take another look at the book showing where the old riverbed might be.

Once he was home his family were amazed to hear of the prospective journey – his mother saying that it was quite an honour for him to be chosen to accompany the old man – normally Alton travelled alone.

It was tough for Tan to get to sleep that night, his head was whirling with everything that had happened to him. Firstly, there was the dragon. The whole reason for him climbing up the mountain that rose high above the castle was that Otto had said there were stories of people seeing something large flying high near the mountain top and that was what he had been dared to investigate.

He was very much looking forward to visiting with the beast again.

Then he pondered on what had changed the relationship between him and Otto, he just couldn't think of any reason for the other lad to turn against him and he missed the companionship of the other boy.

After that there was his pleasure at the thought of the picnic with Autumn and finally the prospect of his journey with Alton.

How his usually quiet life was changing.

CHAPTER FOUR

OTTO

He could remember to the day when his feelings for Autumn changed. The three friends were walking down the track from the castle when the sun had popped its head from out behind a cloud and Autumn's head of hair became a glow of coppery silk. She'd turned her face up to the sun which reflected against her skin giving it a radiance as she laughed at some joke or other that Tan had cracked. Otto's jaw had almost hit the ground – gosh, she was so beautiful, how had he never noticed before. He'd pulled himself back together and walked alongside her becoming more aware of the rapport between Tan and her. Another thing he'd never noticed – why couldn't she look at him like that!

Inside he seethed as Autumn's focus seemed totally fixed on Tan and the conversation they were having. Otto felt like a total outsider, and it wasn't a nice feeling. Tan was supposed to be his best friend so surely he must realise what he was doing?!

As he dropped behind them he began to formulate a plan – a challenge, in fact!

CHAPTER FIVE

AUTUMN

Having braided her long auburn hair to keep it from flicking into her face on her ride, Autumn brushed Blackberry's coat ensuring that he looked in his usual pristine condition for their outing. She picked out any clods of muck caught in his feet and once he was spic and span she turned her attention to his tack, making sure that was all in order.

"Ponies take a lot of looking after," she told Blackberry. "But you're worth it!" He nickered back at her taking pleasure in hearing her voice.

Footsteps shuffled on the gravel just outside the stall and she looked up trying not to groan when she saw who it was.

"Where are you off too?" Otto asked as soon as he was close enough not to shout.

"Just for a ride over the fields as usual," she answered

calmly, feeling relieved that she'd already packed the picnic away out of sight. At least he wouldn't spot that there was food enough for more than one person.

"Would you like some company? I can walk with you if you don't go too fast."

"That's kind of you Otto, but Blackberry enjoys the freedom of a good fast trot and canter."

As he stared forlornly at his feet, she almost felt sorry for him but there was no way he could come – his treatment of Tan recently had been appalling.

She tightened the girth and led the pony out into the open, grabbing the rucksack of food and drink as she passed. Once settled comfortably in the saddle with a wave of her hand she set Blackberry off at a trot down the lane. Normally she would have preferred to walk for a while to warm the pony's legs up a bit first, but she wanted to put as much distance between herself and Otto as soon as possible.

"I wish he'd take the hint and leave me alone," she muttered to herself.

At the end of the lane, she slowed Blackberry down to a brisk walk and checked behind her. As Otto was standing where she'd left him staring after them, she headed in the opposite direction of where she really wanted to go in case he decided to follow on foot. Once they were out of sight, she turned in a big circle and urged Blackberry into a canter towards the rendezvous point.

The old riverbed was quite obvious now that they knew what they were looking for because the plants that grew in it were green and verdant.

"It must be more fertile here," Autumn said as she

poked a finger into the earth. "Look, the soil is loamy compared to that over there."

The picnic was a great success. They sat next to where the old river had run before it had been forced to change course, chatting comfortably with one another.

"You're so lucky to be able to get away from the village but I'll miss your company. Just think I'll have to put up with Otto!"

Tan laughed out loud, flattered to hear that she enjoyed being with him rather than with Otto.

"He's always hanging about trying to speak to me and it's hard work to have a proper conversation as he has no idea what to say. It never used to be like that. You and I don't seem to have that problem. What has caused the rift between the two of you?"

A beam spread across Tan's face as he answered, "I have no idea why he's decided to treat me as the enemy, but I feel just the same as you, when I'm with you it's as if I can say anything I want to and you'll understand."

"The three of us were a team. Have you any idea how many times we got into the castle by climbing up that old rowan tree?" Tan laughed, "It was such fun wasn't it and most of the time no-one else was even aware we were there with Otto roaming about the castle. Such a shame those times have gone and for a reason we don't know."

After a comfortable silence he told her about the dragon.

"A dragon?! How come I've never seen it? And it speaks to you?! Wow!"

"Just think how I felt when it caught me, I was sure I was about to crash to the ground and there's no way I would have survived that! No way at all!"

Autumn's face went ashen.

"I can't bear to think about it! It makes me feel sick!"

"Its cave is so high above the castle that no-one else could know it's there. Don't tell anyone about it because I think the dragon wants its existence kept quiet."

She tapped her heart with a fist, "Of course! You can trust me, you know that!"

He smiled at her.

"So… does the dragon have a name? And how will it know you are waiting for it when it's up in its cave?"

"Hopefully I can find out more if I have time to visit it before my trip." He looked at the sky, "Shame, I think we ought to make a move, it's getting late, see the sun has dropped right down."

"I guess you're right, but I wish we had longer here, it's been fun," she said as she began to gather up the remnants of their picnic.

Once everything was stowed away safely in the bag, Autumn stood beside Blackberry looking at Tan. "You will come and see me before you leave, won't you?"

"Of course!"

Then she leaned forward and pressed her lips to his cheek. "I won't be able to do that when we say goodbye so I'm doing it now. Keep safe!" and she swung herself into the saddle.

Tan was so shocked he didn't move an inch and then put his palm up to his cheek as he stared back at her.

"I will," was all he could say.

CHAPTER SIX

TAN

The pace that Alton set had Tan trotting alongside the mule that the librarian was riding. The saddlebags on her haunches were filled to the brim so the lad had to carry the rest.

He looked back over his shoulder towards the village at the small redhaired figure who was standing staring after them. Next to her was the familiar figure of Otto, along with his mother and sister who were waving frantically.

With one last look he focussed his gaze on the rocky terrain in front of him.

"Alright young man? No regrets I hope."

"None, sir. I am excited to be travelling with you but that's not to say I won't miss my family."

"And a certain young lady too I rather guess."

Tan rubbed his cheek gently. Autumn had been quite correct in her assumption that she wouldn't be able to kiss him when they finally said their goodbyes, and he found that he was quite desperate to feel her lips on his cheek again. Why Otto had come to see Tan off was yet another mystery, but the ex-friend had kept an eagle eye on Tan and Autumn making Tan feel rather uncomfortable. Roselda on the other hand had just laughed knowingly when she saw her brother smile at the redheaded girl.

"Do you know how long the whole journey will take us sir?"

"That will all depend on what obstacles we might come across enroute, but it could be many days, so I hope your new boots are comfortable."

Tan was rather proud of his sturdy but soft leather footwear and the thick socks which the shop owner had promised would help cushion his feet. He had a second pair in his backpack along with a very warm jumper and a spare pair of serviceable trousers. To top it all was a thick waterproof brown cloak.

"Thank you, sir I've never had such good quality gear before."

"Well, I can see the merchant took note of my instructions. It's essential that you have the right clothing for all weathers, or you would be very miserable during our journey – I know because I learned the hard way."

The librarian was sporting much the same clothing as Tan, but what had surprised the young man was that he also had a stout stick resting in a holster between his shoulder blades and Tan's eyes kept flicking towards it wondering quite what its purpose was.

They travelled in silence for a while until Tan looked at his mentor.

"Sir?"

"Yes Tan?"

"I have this weird feeling that we are being watched."

"Well done! You are correct, they have been trying to surround us for quite a while. Now, whatever happens, trust me to handle the situation and make sure you do not get in my way at all," the librarian told him quietly.

"Yes sir."

Tan's eyes flicked from side to side keeping an eye on the men who were now in view and keeping pace with them. They were a rather motley crew, quite dishevelled and rough looking in appearance. They reminded Tan of some men who had recenty caused a rumpus in the village, by all accounts they had thieving on their minds when they'd tried to creep into the castle. They were driven out of the village with a stern warning never to return.

"Get ready!" his master told him. "But, more importantly, remember what I have said about leaving it to me."

The lad braced himself, he had no fighting skills whatsoever, but he would try if push came to shove.

As one, the men began to close in on them shouting instructions to halt or their lives would be forfeit.

Quick as a flash the librarian grabbed the stout staff from between his shoulder blades and moved the mule in a tight circle.

"Beware!" he called out, "It is not our lives that will be lost but yours if you do not disperse and leave us alone."

The tallest and roughest looking of the men guffawed and indicated to the others to move in.

There was a loud bang as the staff swung about in a big circle and one by one the men dropped to the ground. Tan moved as swiftly as he could out of the way.

"I did warn you!" Alton muttered as he brought the mule to a halt and dismounted. He examined each and every man, using their hair to lift their heads off of the ground. Satisfied that none of them were moving he turned to Tan.

"Well done boy! You were quite quick on your feet."

"Are… are they dead?"

"No, just stunned. It was foolish of them to ignore my warning. They will remain like that for a few hours, if not longer and we can only hope that the animals who live in the forest do not venture out to see what they taste like – but that is not our problem. We have to move on, and swiftly at that, covering our tracks so that when they do awaken they will struggle to follow us."

It seemed like no time at all until Tan was traipsing through a gently running stream, trying to ensure that the water stayed below ankle height so he did not get a boot full of water. When they reached a fork in the stream they split up.

"Keep going until you reach the waterfall and then step onto some of the rocks at one side of it. Stay on the rocks for a few strides until you get to the rough ground which is a short distance off from that point. After that step lightly back to the water and cross to the other bank and do the same on that side. Return to meet me here but do not under any circumstances step out onto the bank at any other time. Alright?"

"Yes sir."

After quite a trek Tan guessed he was nearing his destination and when he turned a bend in the stream he was thrilled to see the water cascading down into a small pool. He'd never seen a waterfall before and he stood for a long time just enjoying watching and listening to it. It was a soothing sound and he wished they were camping nearby so it could lull him into sleep. After a while, he followed his instructions stepping out onto the rocks on one side of the waterfall.

Back at the meeting point there was no sign of Alton or Dora, the mule, so he stood obediently in the stream where the water was at its lowest and waited. Although his boots were wet on the outside, it was a relief to find that no moisture was seeping through to his feet.

He listened to the noises around him, breathing in the smells of the flowers growing along the water's edge as a gentle breeze rustled their leaves. Birds were singing happily away to one another busy collecting grubs and suchlike for their dinner.

Eventually another sound interrupted Tan's thoughts – the sploshing of the mule as it trod through the water.

"Good, you are here. Did you step out of the stream at all?"

"No sir, I made sure I stayed in the water apart from where you told me to tread. Can I ask why?"

"If those brigands do decide to follow us, we are laying a false trail for them. They will know we entered the stream but will have no idea which way we have gone. It is only if they find your footprints either side of the waterfall and those of the mule where we left the water down the other fork that they will think they have found the direction that we have gone in. Now we will go back the way we came as there is a pathway we can take which will hide any traces of us being there."

"Have you done this before, sir?"

"Oh yes, many times – my mentor was an expert at fieldcraft. I hope that by the time we return to the village you will have a good knowledge of it too."

"There appears to be much more to this man than just a librarian," Tan thought to himself. "I might like to know how to do what he did to those men."

CHAPTER SEVEN

AUTUMN

She was bored, even practising her already largely perfect archery skills hadn't improved her mood. Otto, try as he might, didn't have the conversational skills of his ex-friend so definitely couldn't fill Tan's shoes, which was strange when she considered the fact that Otto was the son of the Lord and Tan's mother took in sewing from the villagers.

Otto was currently engaged with his family and some visitors who had arrived earlier that day so Autumn knew she would be free to roam wherever she wished without coming across him.

What should she do?

She had a yen to try and find Tan's dragon. It would be fascinating to have a conversation with one.

Not at all sure whether the dragon would consider Blackberry as fodder, she went on foot.

The trek up the winding road seemed quite far for someone who nearly always travelled by pony but by the time she arrived at the plateau she was only slightly out of breath, having stopped just the one time beside a large oak tree. Settling herself onto a nearby boulder the red-haired girl pondered how to get the dragon's attention.

"Shall I shout, or whistle? Maybe clap my hands? Who knows how well a dragon can hear? What I am not going to do is climb up the rocks because I am not nearly as agile as Tan."

In the end she decided to put a finger either side of her mouth and give a shrill but loud whistle. Again… and again.

After another whistle she found herself nearly batted over by the updraft of huge wings as the stunning beast landed behind her. Its body was the size of a big horse.

"I am not a dog to be summoned at will!" the fierce voice said into her head making her jump.

"Thank you for coming," she answered politely. "Oh my… you are absolutely beautiful!"

The dragon was a deep rust colour and its scales gleamed in the sunlight.

"So… very… amazing!"

The beast appeared to preen in the glory of the compliment as it turned its head to admire the overlapping scales across its body.

"I can't believe I am speaking to a dragon!" Autumn said breathlessly. "And, I nearly forgot! I've brought you something which I believe you like!" From her pocket she pulled out a handful of acorns and scattered them on the ground a little way from where the dragon stood.

"I have seen you from afar with the boy – you have hair the same colour as my scales," responded the dragon.

"My name is Autumn, because of it. Do you have a name?"

The dragon studied her thoughtfully.

"He did not ask that."

"Tan, or rather Tancred is my friend and told me all about you. He did come back to try and see you, but you weren't here and he wanted to let you know that he has had to go away for a while but looks forward to meeting you again on his return."

"Hmm," the beast's golden eyes studied her closely.

There was silence between them although not an uncomfortable one as they studied one another and then he delicately sucked up one of the acorns she had strewn across the ground before responding, "Dragons do not call themselves names, so you can name me whatever you wish, so long as it isn't something like Spot the dog!"

She giggled before asking, "Could I… would you mind… can I touch your scales please?"

"Yes," came the short answer and he lowered his great head.

She put a tentative hand out and gently stroked it over the burnished copper shiny scales which overlapped all the way over his head, neck and body. They were surprisingly soft and felt quite malleable, a bit like worn leather. Each scale fitted perfectly beneath another.

"Shining Leaves!" she announced, "That suits you down to the ground because your scales are like leaves, but for short I will call you Leaf. Is that acceptable to a proud dragon like you?"

An almost human nod was his agreement as he reached across and touched her hair briefly.

"Strange, why do most humans have this?"

"Maybe to keep our heads warm," she laughed back at him.

"I would like to hear more about humans and their lives so will you keep visiting me? I watch from afar and you are not at all like dragons."

She giggled at the thought and then replied, "Of course, I'd love to, but it would be easier if I could ride my pony, Blackberry here but would you want to eat him?"

A laugh resounded in her head as he answered, "No, I would not eat your pet, but you must swear not to let other humans know of my existence, although you may speak to Tancred about me if you so wish."

"Consider it done. Now, how do I get your attention so that you will know that I am here to see you?"

"Your whistle is very loud and if I am not busy, I will come. Bring acorns with you because fresh acorns are very tasty!" he ordered.

* * *

Autumn held her head high as she marched back home down the sloping road sometime later. She had chores to do but she was tingling all over with excitement at having spoken to a dragon. She couldn't wait to tell Tan all about it. Even the sight of Otto waiting for her outside the stable didn't dull her pleasure.

"I thought you had visitors and had to remain with them?"

"They have gone to bathe and dress before dinner so I thought I would slip out for a while."

"Are they family?"

He grunted as if he wasn't happy, "It's my uncle – my father's younger brother, Jasper. They've never got on as my uncle is very resentful of the fact that as the elder sibling my father automatically is Lord of this castle and everything that goes with it. Jasper was gifted a sizeable house with land some distance away."

"Why isn't he happy with that? It's more than a lot of people have."

"He believes he would make a better Lord of the castle and has always felt that way, so they argue a lot when he's here about the way my father runs everything. It can be... quite tiring!"

"But you are next in line, aren't you?"

"I believe so. My father has been training me to take over whenever that time comes."

"And you'd like that?" Autumn asked watching his face closely to see if she could read his mind.

"It will be a challenge, but I think I can do it. We'll just have to see."

Autumn couldn't remember them ever having such a long conversation, but he'd obviously had enough of the subject because he said, "You look rather pleased with yourself, where have you been?"

She shrugged, "Not far, just for a stroll," and with that she set to mucking out Blackberry's stall, her daily chore.

The lad just stood and watched and then offered to help.

"No thank you, I prefer to do this on my own, I enjoy it."

"How can you enjoy cleaning up horse poo?" he jeered.

"I enjoy everything that has to do with looking after my pony," she retorted as she scooped another forkful of muck into the wheelbarrow.

"Weird! We have stable boys to do that."

"You would, after all you live in a castle and have a totally different way of life to me – me being the blacksmith's daughter!"

"Would… would you want to live in a castle?" Otto was blushing when she looked up at him.

"Oh no, that is not the kind of life that would suit me at all!"

"How do you know when you've never tried it?"

"Nor do I have any wish to do so, I have other ideas of what would suit me – I am sure many other girls would yearn for such a life but the thought of having servants at my beck and call and meeting and greeting people from other lands has no appeal for me. Anyhow, I love caring for Blackberry and I would hate anyone having to do it for me."

Otto stared back looking rather annoyed, "So, you want to be a village girl all of your life?!" he spat out.

"Don't be so angry Otto, your temper often gets the better of you. You were born to be a Lord but I know my path in life is totally different from that, and you just have to accept it. We make our own destiny, Otto, that is what I believe."

Without a further word the lad stormed off obviously not at all happy about the answers she had given him.

"Oh dear! I think I may have upset him, but he needs to know how I feel. I will not be living in the village for the rest of my life, I have always known that."

31

CHAPTER EIGHT

OTTO

He felt as if he'd been flattened by a herd of elephants! His rival was no longer on the scene yet it seemed that Autumn would have no desire to live in the castle – in fact from the look of it, no interest in Otto himself, but then she'd never been one to take notice of whether one was high born or a villager, she treated them all as equals.

His shoulders drooped as he trudged home, the anger that he'd felt dropped away from him. He should have had more sense than to imagine someone as beautiful as her could feel anything for him.

What's more he was missing his best friend – what a fool he'd been! He just hoped that Tan was enjoying travelling with the librarian.

CHAPTER NINE

TAN

As their stew bubbled away over the fire, Alton had Tan doing various stretches and holding poses which he explained were good for building up the lad's strength and stamina.

"You must do these same forms every day, rain or shine and I will add to them once you have them perfected."

"Sir."

The librarian then looked straight into Tan's eyes his face deeply serious.

"You have told me that you wish to learn all that I know, do you swear to keep my teachings to yourself and follow my instructions to the best or your ability?"

Very briefly Tan wondered what he had got himself into because to be honest he had no idea what Alton really was other than a librarian, but his gut told him he should agree, and he found those kind of feelings did not usually lead him astray.

"Yes, sir, I swear."

"In that case from now on you are, let us say, my apprentice and you should call me Master."

"Yes, Master."

"We'll eat and then we will search for some wood to make you a staff, there is still plenty of light for us to do that."

"But… as a librarian's assistant why would I need one?"

The man smiled back at him.

"Why, to protect yourself of course!"

After their meal they left the mule by the camp and began to search for a branch that was of a good length.

"Will this do, Master?" Tan held up a long branch that had broken away from a tree.

"No Tan, we need a green sapling, because that will have life running through it, in fact this one here is perfect!"

The apprentice stood beside the master expectantly assuming that Alton would be the one to wield the rather lethal looking knife which he had in his hand.

"You must be the one to cut it… and why do you think that should be the case?"

"I have no idea, Master."

"It is so that your own magic will mingle with the sapling's magic and that will bind you to it."

"Does… does that mean that I couldn't use your staff if there was a need for me to do so?"

"Hmm… that is an interesting question and has a rather complicated answer. You could swing it about, but it would not be anything other than a stick to you… however, if you were wielding it to protect me then the magic could possibly kick in. Let's hope we never have to test that theory out."

Tan looked shocked but obediently took hold of the weapon and began to cut the sapling – it went through it like a knife through butter.

At the very moment that the young tree broke away from its root he sensed a wave of energy shoot up his arm and he dropped the knife.

"Ah, now you can see what I mean," Alton smiled. "Take a good hold of it with both hands. How does the length seem to you?"

"Just right."

"You will need to spend time smoothing it down to ensure there are no splinters or rough patches and look, just there by your feet there is the perfect stone to do just that. When you work with it close your eyes and allow your senses to guide you in how you want the staff to feel and look – every staff is different as is each person. I realise you find that a strange concept but trust me, it is so."

"Yes, Master."

"I do not envisage the brigands being able to find us now, so please can you gather some more dry fuel for the fire and build some bracken up for each of us to have a bed to lie in."

They had travelled a good distance since the attack and although he wouldn't admit it, Tan was feeling rather weary and even the thought of a bed made of leaves and twigs sounded wonderful. It would act as a buffer between their bodies and the cold earth and so it was with a glad heart that he set about his chores, whistling to himself as he did.

After a while his Master told him, "I will leave you here while I go and set some snares to catch a couple of rabbits for our meal tomorrow night. You can start work on the staff."

Once Alton had left Tan set himself down on the ground with his back against a nearby tree and ran his hands up and down his new staff. It felt comfortable in his hands. Then he began working to get the notches out of it.

He was so absorbed in using the smoothing stone for some time he didn't notice his master's return to the fireside or that night had fallen.

"You have done well, young man, but time for bed or you'll be too exhausted to travel tomorrow."

The lovely leafy smell of the "mattress" meant that sleep came quickly but then so it seemed did the dawn chorus. The melodic singing of the birds woke Tan who was greatly relieved to see that Alton too, was only just stirring. He didn't want to appear lazy on his first morning in his new role of apprentice.

After a quick breakfast of bread and cheese, Alton went to see to his snares and came back with a pair of coneys which he gutted, wrapped in an oiled cloth and hung at the back of his saddle. Then they set off at a good steady pace. Whenever they stopped for a rest Tan would work with his new staff until it made his fingers ache, but he could see the effort was worthwhile as the wood gradually became more tactile and pleasant to hold.

The idea of using magic was a totally new one to him, something he had never considered during his short life.

As dusk began to fall, they stopped to make camp and

Tan was told to gather bedding once he had set up the fire. Then he had to practice the stretching exercises.

Over a roasted rabbit dinner, Alton admired the lad's handiwork with the staff.

"It looks as if you have nearly finished," he pronounced. "Once you're satisfied with it you need to decide how you want to form the head, I would recommend something simple which will be comfortable to hold. Remember though that even when it is finished you will have to constantly keep handling the staff so that it will recognise you as its owner."

Tan's eyes widened at that comment. "You make it sound as if it is alive."

"Think of it as if you have magic in you that needs to transfer to your staff."

"Yes, Master."

"I can give you some soothing cream you can put on those blisters before you go to bed," Alton said as he damped the fire down to keep the embers burning throughout the night.

Tan found the bracken bed that he'd made quite comfortable and was soon nodding off nicely. An owl hooted loudly nearby, but not enough to disturb him and neither did the whimper of some animal not too far away.

He awoke early having slept well. He still felt warm and cosy almost as if he had a hot water bottle but as he stretched his eyes popped open in alarm – something that gave out heat was slumbering right next to him!

CHAPTER TEN
AUTUMN

There had been no sight or sound of Otto since their conversation although Autumn did feel rather concerned that she might have upset him too much, for all that she was quite relieved not to have to make the stilted conversation that always occurred nowadays.

Once the lessons were over, she saddled up Blackberry, grabbed her bow and slung the quiver of arrows across her back and set off, heading back up in the direction of where Shining Leaves lived. Enjoying the warmth of the sun beaming down on her back and shoulders, Autumn let her mind wander thinking mainly about Tan and wondering how he was getting along. It was surprising quite how much she missed him.

As they neared the plateau there was a rush of wind as the dragon circled above them. She soothed Blackberry telling him it was a friend and not to worry and because the animal was such a steady one, he settled back into a walk while keeping a sharp eye on the dragon which was now landing not far in front of them.

"Well met, Leaf! It's good to see you."

The sunlight bounced off of the gleaming scales on his body as he inclined his head in a rather regal fashion, eyeing up the pony.

Blackberry snorted gathering himself up in preparation to flee from what appeared to be a huge predator.

"It's OK, Blackberry. Leaf! Are you able to communicate with him to let him know you're not going to attack and eat him please?"

The dragon must have done just that because Autumn felt the pony relax beneath her.

She dismounted and tied the reins to one of the stirrups but loose enough to allow the animal to graze, he wouldn't stray far anyway.

Settling herself down on a grassy knoll Autumn proceeded to tell Shining Leaves about her day and then, much to her great surprise, how much she missed Tan.

The dragon was a good listener and took it all in.

In turn, he asked her what humans had inside their rather flimsy looking homes. When she explained he snorted with amusement, puzzled as to why they would need a bed and a range to cook their food on.

Then she asked him where he had flown to that day.

It seemed that he had been quite a distance and at one point he'd seen Tan and Alton far below – he'd been so high up in the clouds they would have thought he was just a bird.

"Do they seem alright?" she asked anxiously. "Could you tell?"

The dragon's laughter echoed in her head as he soothed her concerns.

She felt the humour die away as he tipped his scaly head to one side and then the other as if giving some matter or other some great thought.

"Is something bothering you, Shining Leaves?"

"There is trouble coming this way… and soon."

"How could you know?"

"There is a ripple in the weave of the magic that is all around us, I cannot really explain it to a human such as you."

Autumn gave him a fierce glare. "Try! If the villagers need to ready themselves for a fight, then I should let them know! Where does the magic come from?"

"It is all around us but where the epicentre of the ripple is, I cannot tell apart from the fact that it is getting closer."

* * *

Riding at a leisurely pace back home Autumn pondered on the dragon's words. How to warn the villagers so that they could prepare for trouble? That was the question.

Shining Leaves had promised to keep scouring the surrounding countryside and would send a warning if he sighted anything that would help. For her part Autumn was to keep vigilant just in case she spotted any unusual happenings.

After shooting at the targets that were set up for her archery practice, she returned home and settled Blackberry down in his stall making sure she picked out his feet to ensure they were clean and empty of any stones.

"You were amazingly brave today!" she said giving him a big kiss on the end of his velvety soft nose. He was more interested in the fact that he knew his bucket of food was just outside and kept looking over towards it.

CHAPTER ELEVEN

OTTO

His anger at Autumn had long subsided as he readied himself for the forthcoming banquet – yet another one in honour of his uncle's arrival at the castle. Straightening his formal clothing and ensuring it was pristine, he stepped into the corridor catching sight of a glimpse of gold at the edge of his vision. Of course, it wouldn't be Autumn. Then another thought popped into his head in that she would never be accepted easily into the society of the court within the castle, being deemed far to lowly and that hurt him. Why should a person's birth standing make such a difference? The wearer of gold continued heading towards him and he realised it was his uncle's ward, Yulia approaching. The dress she was wearing floated around her legs as she moved much as if she was dancing.

Her soft voice called to him, "How good to see you, I haven't seen much of you since we arrived. Can we walk to the banqueting hall together?"

"I would be more than happy for the company," he responded, dropping into the natural and polite manner that had been instilled into him, whilst noticing that she smelled quite delightfully of orange blossom. "How have you occupied yourself today?"

She laughed gently, "Well… I have been to the library but was disappointed to find the librarian has already left on his travels. He is a very interesting person to speak to, I've discovered from my past visits here."

"He is that… I quite agree. One of my friends has been apprenticed to him for quite a while."

At that thought, his stomach sank, as he considered yet again his recent actions towards Tan. They were not how one should treat a friend!

"You look a little sad, is there something bothering you Otto?"

"My lady, I am sorry, just a small reminder of something I must put right when I am able to," he replied forcing his attention back to her, "And how has my uncle been treating you?"

"Well… you know how your uncle is… he likes to keep matters close to his chest, not like your father who is totally the opposite."

That made the lad laugh because the brothers were like chalk and cheese and his father's amiability was something that made the villagers and staff love him, as opposed to his uncle who was rather dour and intimidating.

Putting her hand on his arm to stop him, she looked at him, a serious look on her face.

"He has something up his sleeve, but I know not what – although my gut feeling is that it is not good. He has been spending a lot of time with his newest advisor, a man I do not take to. They stop speaking whenever I have come near to them, as if they are plotting something or other." She hesitated before continuing, "Please Otto, you must keep your eyes and ears open as will I and I will let you know if I have any news."

They continued in silence, a small bead of worry making the Lord's son's stomach tense in anxiety, because he too, had foreboding that something was not quite right, but he had no idea what. It was very surprising that Yulia had spoken against her protector, that took a great deal of courage.

CHAPTER TWELVE

TAN

"Well, well, I've never seen anything like that before!" Alton announced shaking his head in surprise.

"But what is it?" Tan asked his master bemusedly.

"It's a wolf-cat – part wolf and part wild cat and they are extremely rare in these parts," Alton answered.

The wolf-cat began to rub against Tan's legs.

"You should feed her," he said handing Tan some of the leftover rabbit they'd had for their dinner.

The animal gobbled it up, bones and all and the sound that rumbled from its chest was something akin to a very deep purr as its long white tipped tail began to wag from side to side much as a dog's tail would. She was a beautiful colour of slate grey.

"I didn't know anything like this existed," the lad muttered reaching down to her head which was level with his knees to run his fingers all the way down her silky back. He was rewarded with a definite purr. "You're going to grow very big, looking at the size of your paws," he told her.

"As I said, they are exceptionally rare and the fact that it chose to snuggle up to sleep with you is an honour as they are very solitary creatures. The females send them away from a very young age so that they can learn to survive in the wild on their own. They only come together to breed."

Tan ran his fingers along its silky back and it gave out another loud purr. Its body was that of a big cat and its head had the muzzle of a wolf.

"You're rather beautiful," he told it as he passed over some more meat.

"Time to be off!" his master called to him as he saddled up the mule. Tan kicked over the remains of the fire ensuring that it was totally out and then used some bracken to spread the ashes across a large area before he picked up the stones which had acted as a hearth and tossed them into the surrounding bushes.

"Ready!" he answered. "Do you think it will follow us?"

"Time will tell," his master answered kicking the mule into a steady walk.

Looking over his shoulder Tan saw the wolf-cat settle down on its haunches and give a mournful whine watching them until they disappeared from view.

It was hard work trekking through the narrow forest track. Alton told Tan to clear the way in front to make it easier for the mule to get through and every so often he would have to beat at the undergrowth with his staff.

Suddenly there was a loud shout and a big man leapt in front of them brandishing a sword.

"Halt!" he yelled, "Get off that mule old man and hand over your saddle bags and I will spare your lives!"

Realising that he was blocking Alton's view of their aggressor Tan tried to shuffle to one side, but the pathway was too narrow and the bracken and brambles too thick for him to do much and when he turned to look at his master there was no indication from him as to what his apprentice should do.

The man pushed his way towards the lad and grabbed him, spinning him around and laying the sword against his neck.

"I said, get off the mule, old man! Are you deaf? I will cut the boy's throat if you do not obey me!"

Tan felt the sword make a small cut in his neck and he could feel blood beginning to trickle down his neck.

"Okay, okay, just wait a minute. As you have rightly said, I am old, and my bones are a bit creaky, so it takes time." Tan was too panicky even to smile when he thought how agile Alton was normally.

As his master began to swing his leg over the back of the mule there was a roar and the wolf-cat sprang out of nowhere leaping onto the assailant's back, flattening him. Tan found himself trapped by the heavy weight of the man on top of him as he felt the rasp of a rough tongue lick his chin.

"Get up then!" Alton called.

"He's a bit of a dead weight and I can't move."

"Don't be so feeble! Just roll him off of you."

"Can't you help me please?"

"There's not room but I'm sure you'll find a way."

By the time Tan was finally on his feet he was panting, the wolf-cat purring loudly and curling itself around his legs.

"Thank you, my friend!" he said giving the animal a rub from head to toe. "Thank you!"

The purring increased.

"It seems that you have a new admirer and now you have your answer as to whether she would follow us."

He passed over a piece of rabbit to Tan which the wolf-cat took gently from his hand.

"How many cubs do they have in a litter?"

"I have read that it is usually between two and ten, but how many of those actually survive is unknown. I have only ever seen them in illustrations in books in the library. Perhaps you should communicate with her and build up a bond, much like the one you are working on with your staff. Give her some more food though, she deserves it." Then the Master uttered a gruff, "On we go. No time to waste chatting!"

After a few hours of hiking down the narrow track it finally led into a small mossy green area surrounded by trees, the wolf-cat remaining at Tan's heels.

"This looks a good place for us to rest our weary heads."

Tan didn't need telling twice, quickly gathering kindling, laying the fire and sorting out bedding for them to sleep on. He was hungry and tired. Although his staff was leaning against a tree trunk there was a weird kind of feeling he could sense it wherever he was within the camp.

Shrugging his shoulders, trying to shake off the oddness his thought was that, "Maybe that's what Alton meant by building a bond."

The fire crackled away nicely as he leant his back against a tree watching the pot of rabbit stew bubble away gently. A soft nose touched his leg and then the wolf-cat gave a big yawn and settled herself against his leg.

"You're a real beauty young lady," he told her. "Thank you for coming to the rescue the way you did."

She gave a throaty purr as if she understood him which encouraged him to continue speaking to her as he worked away at his staff. Basically, it was finished but he enjoyed the way it felt beneath his hands, smooth and tactile and… almost alive.

He told the wolf-cat about his life in the village, his friendship with Otto and how he found that he missed Autumn much more than he would have expected to. The kiss also came up and when he mentioned that the wolf-cat looked up at him purring before touching her soft muzzle to exactly the same spot that Autumn's lips had.

CHAPTER THIRTEEN

AUTUMN

"Autumn!" a voice whispered urgently from the bushes. "Autumn! Please hear me!"

"What is it Otto that's so important?"

She could hear the panic in his tone.

"There's been a coup within the castle! My father has been imprisoned by my uncle!"

"What?!! Are you sure?" and she turned to face where his voice was coming from and then moved down next to him.

"Oh yes!"

"But aren't you in danger as the eldest son?"

"I should be alright. I know where to hide and anyway he just thinks I am the feeble son. He has forgotten that I am the Lord's heir. Look, we don't have time to talk about this – I need to return to the castle and consider what I can do to keep our people safe. Trust me, I can stay out of trouble but you on the other hand must run. It's too late to get word to the villagers as my uncle's soldiers are already amongst them rounding them up."

"But… but my parents?"

"They should be spared because there is not another blacksmith for miles around. Your mother too, as a teacher will be useful. But you…" his voice wobbled, "you are in danger. Find somewhere safe to hide and then perhaps you could try and catch up with Tan and Alton, they will know what to do."

The closest that Autumn had got to talking to her parents about possible troubles in the village was to ask them what would happen if they were attacked, but she had never considered that the uncle would be the person causing it.

Her father had guffawed with laughter, "What on earth put that into your tiny little mind, lass? That's exactly what the Lord's soldiers are supposed to guard us against."

Glancing up at her mother she saw a worried expression flash across her face that was gone within moments.

Autumn felt her stomach almost drop to the ground and then she stiffened up with resolve.

"Thank you, Otto for the warning."

Otto's head tipped to one side as he listened to the noise of many feet coming up the hill towards them, the soldiers shouting commands at their prisoners.

"They come! Go now and keep safe, Autumn. Please ask Tan's forgiveness if you see him. I was wrong in how I treated him before he left, but at least he is safely out of range with Alton."

"You keep safe as well," and she gave him a gentle peck on his forehead, feeling strangely reassured about him

51

because he sounded more like a Lord's son than the usual Otto.

It was a matter of moments before she had led Blackberry into the dense and tall bushes that grew below the road. She put a finger against his nose and told him to be silent. His response was a gentle snort as if he understood.

There was nothing else to do but wait with a knocked arrow in her hand in case they were discovered.

The soldiers were not gentle with the villagers pushing and shoving them in an effort to hurry them along. Some of the villagers had blood on them and she could see purple welts on their arms and faces as if they had been beaten. It was not a large village so there were only about thirty people shuffling up the hill some of them pulling crying children along beside them. Tan's mother and sister were in the midst of them.

Autumn felt tears run down her cheeks when she spotted her own parents walking proudly encouraging the others as they did so. When they reached the bend in the track, she felt her mother's gaze sweep back to exactly where Autumn was hidden and a prickle went up the back of her neck, as a voice whispered in her head, "Keep safe, my darling!"

"How could she know I am here?" the girl muttered.

Her mother's hand flicked up as if she was saying goodbye and Autumn blew her a kiss. Surprisingly, even though her mother couldn't have seen her through the foliage she touched her cheek as if the kiss had reached her before a guard pushed at her shoulder and she turned to speak to one of the children nearby trying to quieten them.

"What on earth should I do?" she sobbed burying her face against her pony's warm neck.

* * *

Much later that night when the moon was high in the sky a dragon circled above the village his eaglelike gaze watching the scene below him.

Autumn jimmied the lock on the back door to the merchant's shop with shaking fingers. It went against the grain to break in because she had been taught that stealing was wrong, but she needed to take the necessary clothing for her journey into the unknown.

She was going to try and catch up with Tan and Alton.

The door opened, the hinges squeaking loudly as she pushed it ajar standing stock still and hoping that the sound wouldn't be heard by the guards that she knew were currently enjoying free drinks in the bar that was immediately next door to the merchant's store.

No movement nearby could be heard, and she let out a sigh, hopefully they were too engrossed in their free ales.

Normally she would take time to inhale the gorgeous smells around her but there was no time for that. The moon cast shadows across the shop as she crept forward gradually gathering waterproof and warm clothing, trying to replicate that which she had seen Tan wearing when he left – some stout boots, a couple of thick jumpers which she wanted to sink her face into and socks. Coming across a good-sized waterproof rucksack she realised it would be perfect for her to carry along with some supple leather saddle bags. She knew that she had sufficient spare tack in the stables just in case something needed to be replaced during her journey.

Firelighters and firesticks were added to the purloined goods, a sturdy sou'wester, and sleeping bag which rolled up into a small ball. Then there was a rainsheet which could be fashioned into a tent if tied to a tree or bush.

Moving on she surveyed the dried meats in the food section, choosing carefully what would be filling without taking up too much space.

At long last she hoped she'd collected sufficient for her needs and after a quick glance around the shop making sure that she'd left nothing out of place, she exited the same way she'd entered.

"Shame I can't lock the door behind me, but I guess those greedy guards will soon be looting the place." She could hear them carousing away in the nearby inn, obviously well into their cups.

The next stop was the stables. Water bottles which would hang next to the saddle bags, along with a brush for Blackberry and a hoofpick for his feet. Some hard feed to give him energy was essential too, although he could supplement this with grass.

Finally, she entered the house.

"This could be the last time I come here," she thought trying hard to banish the sadness which threatened to engulf her as she looked through the pantry. The aroma of fresh bread made her think of her mother who would always hum a tune as she kneaded the dough. The loaf would make a welcome addition to her stores.

A dash up to her room had her collecting underwear and other bits and bobs and then she opened the small trunk at the end of her bed, at the very bottom were the daggers which her father had made for her, teaching her how to throw them should she ever be attacked. She secreted them around her body before changing into her newly acquired clothing adding a short sword which fitted nicely into a leather scabbard strapped around her waist.

Time to leave.

With a last longing look around her she arranged the pebbles which were on a window ledge into the shapes which was how she had always let her mother know that she was going out exploring on Blackberry. It was a secret code they used between them, and she knew that if her mother was allowed to return to her home, she would understand that her daughter had been here.

The door clicked quietly behind her as she slipped into the shadows outside the stables.

The dragon's voice echoed into her head, "Be quick, there are soldiers coming!"

CHAPTER FOURTEEN

OTTO

Thank goodness he'd been able to warn Autumn before the soldiers captured her – his only concern was that she would now be going into danger – the forest was something they were warned to stay away from. Now, though he had other more pressing worries… how to keep everyone as safe as possible, including his father, while they tried to work out a way to oust his uncle.

He had to think!

He took the route that the three friends had always used to get back into his rooms by climbing up the old tree beside the window he always kept open in his bathing room.

CHAPTER FIFTEEN

TAN

"You need a name, wolf-cat," he told the purring animal as she pushed her body against his legs enjoying the sensation of his fingers running down her back.

He gave it some thought, "Alpha! That's what I shall call you!" The beast purred even louder as if she approved.

"Tan! Time for you to do your stretches and then we shall spar!" Tan's Master called over to him.

The wolf-cat gave her friend a quick look before slinking off silently into the surrounding bushes.

It was a hard lesson, but through it all Tan felt that his link to the staff was improving. For all that, his body seemed to be black and blue mainly due to the fact that he was still mastering how to shield himself from the blows which constantly came his way.

"Better!" Alton told him encouragingly, "we might yet make a warrior of you!"

It was a relief to bathe in the icy stream running not far away from where they had camped that night knowing that although the cold made his body tingle, it would help diminish any swelling which might occur.

By the time he had returned to the camp site Alton had tidied everything away, leaving some bread and cheese for Tan and the lad's bedding which was always his responsibility.

After a quick but very welcomed bite to eat, Tan brushed away all signs that they had been camping there and then jogged up to walk beside the mule.

"You'll be pleased to know that tonight you will have the luxury of a proper bed as we will be staying over in the next village. You need to keep your eyes and ears open while we are there to try and pick up any bits of news that you can. I will be joining the village elder for dinner and while I am with him you are to eat in the inn where I have booked us two rooms," Alton looked down at the quick smile that crossed his apprentice's face.

"Yes, Master."

Tan looked around them, where was Alpha?

Alton read his mind, "The wolf-cat is keeping her distance from us now. She senses that we're getting closer and closer to civilisation and humans are generally anathema to her kind."

* * *

The main room at the inn was quite full when Alton led them over to where the very rotund barkeep was wiping down the worktop with a rather grubby looking rag.

"Good evening, Mister Drayton," Alton said politely holding out his hand which was gripped by two very meaty fists as the red-faced publican smiled back delightedly.

"How good to see you Master Alton! It's certainly been a while."

"Yes, that it has." He nodded his head towards Tan as he added, "And this is my new apprentice, Tancred."

Tan could see the questions racing through the red-cheeked man's mind as he peered back at him.

"I don't believe we've ever seen you with an apprentice before."

"No, he is the first, but I thought it was time I taught someone else the delights of working in the castle libraries that I tend to visit from time to time – after all, I won't be around for ever!" Tan was fascinated by the wobbling belly of the man as the two adults laughed agreeably with one another.

"Is my usual room available, and the one adjoining it?"

"Of course it is! Are you dining here this evening too? We have a venison stew bubbling away in the kitchen with tatties and greens to go with it."

"Delightful as it sounds, I'm afraid I am expected at the Elder's home this evening, however I'm happy to say that my young apprentice will be able to partake of your excellent fare. I would ask though that you don't let him supp too much of your amazing homebrew because I would like his head to be totally clear in the morning or he will be of no use to me whatsoever."

* * *

As it happened, despite the inn's rather dowdy appearance, the hot food was excellent. It made a really nice change to eat something that was not the rabbit, cheese or the dried meat that they'd had to eat enroute. Pudding was a real treat too, lots of hot custard with a pie.

Tan felt quite relaxed as he soaked up the atmosphere in the room while watching the rather buxom waitress going about her business. He sat with his back against the far wall having made sure he positioned himself in a perfect place to view the whole area. A rather motley crowd of people were enjoying themselves and if anyone got too rowdy then the barkeep would bustle over to them and have a quiet word to keep the noise down.

He wondered how he had come to be a librarian's apprentice now pretending to be a spy.

"Did you hear about the troubles in the village of Wick?" he overheard a man on the next table ask his drinking companion.

"No, what's happened there?"

"The Lord's brother has taken the castle over."

Tan nearly spilt his drink as it neared his mouth and tried not to look like he was listening, despite the beer dribbling down his chin, but he'd obviously failed.

"Young man!", the farmer on the next table called across to Tan. "You seem interested in Wick, do you hale from there by any chance? We've not seen you in these parts before."

"Aye, sir, I do live not too far from the castle. What news do you have about it?"

"Come and join us… you can buy us a drink and I'll let you know everything that I do."

CHAPTER SIXTEEN

AUTUMN

It was quite creepy riding through the dark forest on her own. Blackberry had his ears pricked the whole time as if listening for anything that might be near them. It eased her worry about being alone when every now and then she caught glimpses of Shining Leaves flying just above the tree canopy on the look out for any predators.

Her main task was to ensure that she followed the dragon's lead because he was taking them in the direction of where he had last seen Tan and Alton.

She yawned – it was rare for her to be awake this late in the night.

She swayed from side to side trying not to nod off and it was a great relief when Leaf finally told her to stop and make camp. He would find a way to join her shortly and would keep guard.

In no time at all she had Blackberry hobbled close to a

small stream so that he could drink at will and munch on the grass there. She removed his saddle giving him a quick brush over before putting the saddle next to her bedding roll so that she could use it as a pillow.

There was a crashing noise coming through the trees towards her and she quickly knocked an arrow in her bow, just in case, but it was only the dragon forcing his way through the undergrowth.

"Sleep!" he ordered her. "Have no fear, I will keep watch."

Amazingly as soon as her head touched the saddle, swathed in the warm bedding she was out for the count. It had been an exhausting and certainly an unusual day to say the least.

* * *

A gentle nudge from the dragon's snout woke her and judging from where the sun was in the sky, she deemed that it must be mid-morning.

"Why didn't you wake me sooner? We should be on our way."

"You needed sleep and I thought you would open your eyes when you were ready. I will leave you now to hunt for food."

"Thank you, Shining Leaves I don't know what on earth I would do if you weren't here with us!"

She could have sworn that the dragon smiled back at her before sweeping its tail in a big circle and leaving the camp.

Having checked on Blackberry, she broke into her stores and ate a good-sized breakfast.

"I know I should limit my food but I'm hungry and I didn't get to eat yesterday," she told herself placatingly as she munched on a piece of the bread that her mother had baked. "I guess I'll have to forage for some food and maybe hunt for the odd rabbit or two if I can."

Once her belly felt replete, she refilled the water bottle from the stream, tidied up the camp and brushed Blackberry until he shone, before beetling across to a nearby oak tree to gather handfuls of acorns and thrust them in her pockets – they were to be what Shining Leaves had demanded as payment for his guardianship. A strange request but she was determined to fulfil her end of that bargain. By the time the dragon returned they were ready to set off.

Shining Leaves had already scouted the route ahead of them so at least for now the journey was quite easy.

"Hide!" suddenly came the instruction into her head. "Get off the track!"

It was a scramble to dismount and drag poor Blackberry through the bushes and just in time too, as a horse galloped down the track, its rider bent down low over a neck which was totally covered in lather.

"Lucky that he was going too fast to notice us hidden here," she whispered to Blackberry. "I wonder whose colours he was wearing – they weren't the colours of Lord Travers, that's for sure. I guess he was carrying a message for someone important."

They stayed hidden being quiet as mice. Even Blackberry didn't snort or shuffle about as he normally would have done.

Just as she felt it would be safe to emerge from their cover the dragon's voice echoed in her head.

"You need to find a better hiding place. There are soldiers coming!"

"How long do we have?"

"You must go deeper into the forest, but I will not be able to see you because of the leaves on the trees. Go now!"

"But… where did the rider come from and how come you weren't able to see him until he was nearly upon us?"

"He seemed to come out of nowhere. I will try and track down how that could have happened. Go quickly!"

Autumn stayed on foot so that she could judge where to tread and how to get through the undergrowth safely, the pony close behind her. As they slowly drew away from the main track, she could hear the voices of men calling to one another and she shivered in fear. What if they found her? What would happen?

On the positive side, the men were making so much noise they wouldn't hear them pushing through the bushes.

When the undergrowth became too thick for her to go any further, she led Blackberry behind a huge fallen oak tree, the question was, were they far enough from the track?

"Shame I haven't taught you to drop down on your knees," she muttered to the pony and then to her utter amazement he did just that!

"How… how did you know that's what I needed you to do?" He pressed his soft muzzle against her face as she knelt beside him.

"You are such a clever pony!"

She watched and listened to the men's voices which echoed through the forest as they shouted instructions to one another.

"How far is it to this village called Wick?" one of them called.

"Only a few hours I guess."

Another gruff voice said, "Thank goodness for that. I hope there's somewhere we can wet our whistles – we seem to have been marching for a long time and going through that tunnel was something like a nightmare! We are lucky to have survived."

"I agree, it was a relief to see the daylight as we neared the end!"

Well, that certainly explained why Shining Leaves had been surprised by the arrival of the messenger and the soldiers.

CHAPTER SEVENTEEN

TAN

Tan felt himself being shaken awake. Where was he? He lifted his head from the table and felt the dried drool crack on the side of his mouth. Yuck!

Alton's face moved in and out of focus as he said, "Well, my young apprentice! You appear to have had a good evening!"

With a throbbing head which he really wanted to lay back upon the rather grubby, beer-stained table Tan gazed up at his mentor.

"I'm… I'm sorry sir…" was all he could say as he lurched to his feet and raced out of the inn's door into the cool street to bend over and retch again and again. When he finally straightened up, he spotted a water pump across the street and staggered across to it and forced the handle up and down splashing the icy cold water across his whole head.

That felt a bit better! He thought as he managed to walk steadily back into the bar where Alton was waiting.

"I think you might have enjoyed a little too much of the homebrew," Alton laughed.

Just thinking about that made Tan's stomach gurgle and his head bang.

"Go and sleep it off."

"But... sir, I have news of Wick that I must tell you of."

"It can wait until the morning. I will knock for you so that we can break our fast together and exchange news then."

Morning came far too soon, and this with a still thumping head but Tan dragged himself out of bed as soon as he heard his Master's knock on the door and headed for the communal bathing room. He probably didn't smell very nice gathering from the dried spittle he could still feel on his cheeks.

Dressed in fresh clothing and having washed out his travelling clothes leaving them to dry beside the open window in his room, he met with Alton, pleasantly surprised to find he was hungry enough to eat a huge breakfast which the lady of the inn, Mrs Drayton plumped down in front of him, a knowing smile on her face.

Once she'd left them in peace the librarian told his apprentice to go first with his news.

"It's rather shocking, Master! It seems that Lord Travers' brother has taken over the castle! It sounds like the villagers have all been taken prisoner – I wonder if I should return home to see if there is anything I can do?"

"I too, received this same information from the village Elder yesterday evening who heard it from a merchant

67

about to deliver some goods to the very shopkeeper who supplied you with your clothing. The man was about to enter the village when he saw what was happening. He was lucky because the soldiers were too intent on going about their business rounding up the villagers than paying him any attention. He set up camp in the forest and then crept back to see what was occurring."

"Do… do you think they will have harmed the villagers?"

"I cannot be certain, but my gut feeling is that they would be of more use to the usurper alive than dead." Alton hesitated before going on, "I have information that might be of interest to you."

"What's that? Is it about my mother?"

"No, someone else – a young lady on a pony was seen leaving the village in the dark of the night. The merchant could tell that she and her steed were quite laden."

"Autumn! Thank goodness, she escaped! But where will she be going?" His fingers stroked his cheek as if he could feel where her lips had touched it.

"I would guess she will be trying to find us."

"Is there any way we can help her, Master?"

"We will stay at the inn for another night and then I will leave word of where we are heading in the hope that she arrives here. After all, this is the largest and nearest village to Wick."

Tan looked relieved as he said, "Thank you Sir, that is very thoughtful of you, but should I try and search for her today while we are here?"

"No, lad. That would be quite fruitless, we will continue as I originally planned and find a clearing in the forest to continue with our training. This turn of affairs means that you may need to be proficient with your staff much quicker than I had anticipated."

* * *

Licking her lips presumably enjoying the taste of whatever prey she had just eaten, Alpha lay watching the pair sparring – or rather Alton knocking Tan to the ground again and again and again.

Tan knew better than to complain despite the fact that he felt as if his whole body must be black and blue.

"Protect yourself! Don't just take it!"

It went against the grain for him to raise his staff against his Master but as he rolled in the dirt yet again suddenly, he'd had enough. No more! His body cried out as he stood brandishing his staff out in front of him.

A gleam appeared in Alton's eyes as he brought his own weapon down but… Tan blocked the blow! The lad was so shocked he almost dropped his protective stance, but then he brought his arms up again and pushed back… hard!

"Well done! At last!" Alton cried out. "We'll finish on that good note and in future perhaps you'll remember to never drop your guard and always be prepared for anything."

Tan sank down on his haunches, he was totally done.

"You should feel proud of yourself, apprentice! You came back at me much quicker than I would have expected," and he smiled before he added, "I'll help you apply the tincture to your bruises tonight and maybe you also need to go and relax in a bath full of hot water. That will help."

"Thank you, sir," was about all that the lad could say. The thought of resting in hot water sounded so appealing. "Can I sit here with Alpha for a while to get my breath before I follow you back?"

His Master nodded his agreement adding for him not to sit for too long or his body would sieze up, then he disappeared at speed in the direction of the village.

"How come he is so old, yet so very fit?" Tan murmured to himself as he settled his back against a Rowan tree.

Alpha slid down next to him purring as he traced a gentle hand down her silky pelt. Too many thoughts and worries were racing through his head, and he decided to say them out loud to try and make some sense of them. He told her about the troubles in his village and the fact that his mother and sister were most likely prisoners in the castle, then his concern about Autumn and whether she was safe on her own.

"She's never been out of the village before, rather like me and I have no idea how she will cope."

The animal purred as if she understood and just lay there quietly enjoying his gentle touch.

"I'd better drag myself back to the inn, I guess," he said readying his staff to use to help himself up. The wolf-cat sprung up, her rough tongue rasping against his cheek before she turned and shot off silently into the undergrowth behind them.

"Where's she going at such a pace?" he asked himself as he staggered to his feet. As usual, Alton had been right and now his whole body seemed to have stiffened up, so the thought of the hot bath was very appealing.

CHAPTER EIGHTEEN

AUTUMN

The line of soldiers seemed to go on forever, the sound of their feet reverberating throughout the forest until at long last it was quiet and Autumn felt it might be safe enough to stand up to take a peek about her.

"Well, well, well! What have we here, boys?! We seem to have caught us something of interest!" a sharp scary voice called out as the leaves behind her rustled and branches were pushed aside.

The girl froze, what should she do? The man must have spotted her russet coloured hair above the tree trunk they were hiding behind.

In her head she called out to Shining Leaves in the hope that he could help her.

"Can you flame him?" she asked.

"I can see neither you or him," was the answer. "What's more the fair folk who live in the forest would be very angry if I burned any of the trees."

"What… what should I do?"

No answer from the dragon.

"So, I'm on my own!" Blackberry nudged her leg, "Well, not quite on my own," she thought as she saw the pony readying to scamble to his feet.

She made a signal to him to wait, she needed to see how many men she was going to have to face.

The smirk on the soldier's mouth showed his blackened teeth as he returned her gaze. Looking either side of him she counted five more heads, all of them grinning evilly at her. There were far too many for her to do battle with.

As the soldier's grubby hand stretched out to grab her shoulder, Blackberry lunged to his feet spinning around and lashing out with his hind legs knocking one of the men to the ground. Another one slashed at the pony's rump with a sword and the wound immediately began to bleed.

"Leave him! Please don't hurt him!" Autumn cried.

"We'll do more than that, lassie," the nasty man continued, "we'll feast well tonight! Roasted horse meat! And the same tomorrow too!"

"No! You can't eat him!" Autumn screamed trying to wrest her shoulder out of his grip.

He batted her away as if she was a fly and she splatted down onto the damp leaves.

"Watch us and see, little girl!" Then to his men, "Let's find somewhere where we can light us a good−sized fire boys, my mouth is watering! Scout around can you?" he ordered.

"But sir, shouldn't we catch up with the rest of the platoon?"

A cackle emitted from the leader, "What and share our meal with them – what are you thinking about man! We can be with them tomorrow," hauling Autumn to her feet. Another soldier took hold of Blackberry's bridle and dragged him along slapping him with the side of his sword to make sure he obeyed. The pony bucked and gave an angry squeal.

Autumn was beside herself because gathering from the seriousness of his voice the soldier had every intention of slaughtering her friend. What could she do? Ridiculously she was more worried about Blackberry than herself.

"Shining Leaves! You have to do something!"

Silence reigned from the dragon. He must have abandoned her to her fate.

She dug her heels into the soft ground and tried to pit her weight such as it was against the soldier as he pulled her along behind him, He'd relieved her of the short sword before they'd set off, but he hadn't found the various daggers she had hidden about her person so she set her mind to working out how she could use them against him and win. Surprise was probably the key, but how could she tackle the soldier that had a firm hold of Blackberry's bridle? A shout ahead of them announced that they'd found a spot for them to make camp?

She turned her head sensing that there was something lurking in the undergrowth nearby. Was she imagining it? But there was nothing to see, nothing at all.

Again, she tried to contact Leaf, and tell him they were heading for a clearing, but there was still no answer at all from him.

When the potential camp site came into view Autumn

73

found herself thrown to the ground and tied to a nearby tree.

"Secure the pony so he can't get away!" the soldier ordered his men. "And much more importantly, start laying the fire! I'm drooling at the thought of roasted meat – what a treat!"

It was painful to watch them tipping her stores out onto the ground and whooping with delight at what they found. One of them took the cloak, saying, "You won't be needing this anymore, my love!"

Blackberry shifted from side to side as if trying to free himself, but he was tied too well to do anything.

The leaves nearby moved again but the men were too engrossed in their plunder to notice.

Autumn's heart was in her mouth when she saw them gathering firewood and beginning to lay it out in readiness of cooking their meal and when she saw the knife in one of the men's hand she had to swallow her scream.

CHAPTER NINETEEN

TAN

"There's been no sign of your little lady as yet," Alton mocked Tan, who grimaced.

"I really think I should go and search for her, Master."

His Master replied, "It would be like looking for a needle in a haystack, lad. We wait another day and then we'll move on as planned, but for now let me see you go through your stretches please."

Obediently, Tan began the first of the moves. His body ached all over but at least the ointment that Alton had administered the night before had helped with the bruising. As he had applied it the man had listed the ingredients telling him that at some point in the training they would have to cover how to make potions because you never knew when they would come in handy.

Once stretching was over, Alton began to teach Tan various defensive movements using his staff.

"There are some simple ways you can use the staff when you are about to attack an opponent. Watch and keep them to the forefront of your mind."

It was hard work but, Tan felt he might be improving, albeit slowly. The wolf-cat hadn't made an appearance and he missed her.

"Perhaps she's out hunting again. After all, she seems to have grown in the short time she's been with us and who on earth knows how much food she needs to eat to sustain that growth spurt," he told himself in a much-needed break.

Their own lunch had been provided by the barkeep's wife and was delicious, fresh bread rolls spread with lots of butter and rammed full of cheese. As they ate they discussed Tan's task that evening, which was similar to that of the previous night but Alton's hope was that there would be newcomers in the bar who might have yet more information concerning the situation in Wick.

"But keep off of that lethal homebrew!"

Tan blanched at the thought, "I don't think I want to ever drink that again, Master."

His master laughed, "Time will tell whether you continue to think like that!"

* * *

That evening Tan settled himself again with his back pressed against a wall so that he could survey the room. Alton had gone out, probably to visit the village elder but would return before Tan went to bed.

There were a lot of familiar faces until the door

slammed open as a group of men came in rubbing their hands. Soldiers by the looks of it.

Tan kept an eye on them and hoped they'd sit on the nearby table enabling him to eavesdrop. The colours they were wearing were unfamiliar.

The men jostled one another at the bar, all very keen to get their hands on a drink and the barkeep told them to be patient, he would get to them all as fast as he could. One by one they moved away to stand in front of the blazing fire.

"How much longer do we have to travel? My feet are beginning to get sore!" one of the men grumbled.

"To Wick we go. I reckon it should only take a couple more days."

Tan's ears pricked up as he tried not to smile when the speaker shuffled across and set himself down at the adjacent table. He was soon followed by a few others.

He kept his eyes on the drink that was resting between his hands, trying to look as if he was deep in thought.

"I've not heard of this Wick before, what is there."

"Man… surely you know of the coup that took place there?" a soldier guffawed, "Where has your brain been?"

"You forget, I was sent ahead to scout the land. What coup?"

"The old Lord's brother has taken over the castle and we go there now to receive further orders."

Another soldier piped up, "What difference does it make to us? We fight when we're told and march when we're told, that's the way I see it."

"You're an idiot, we've all been promised a pay rise if we follow the new Lordship, that's what!"

"Where will they get the means for a pay rise? We've been told that before and nuffing has ever come of it."

"Rumour has it that this will be different, the new Lord has much to prove and there is talk that he has set his eyes on other nearby estates too."

"Bah! I'll watch this space!" and the moaning soldier stood up and walked slowly across to the bar to loudly order another drink. "And be quick too, before I die of thirst!"

Tan let his mind ponder on the problems in Wick. How was Otto faring? He missed his old friend – they'd had such good times together before the falling out and he wouldn't want anything to happen to him.

There was silence from the table next to him as the food they'd ordered arrived and they stuffed their faces.

Tan took a small sip of his beer making it last and had been very relieved that the taste of it hadn't turned his stomach. His mind wandered to Alpha wondering where she'd gone.

The talk on the table next to him turned to that day's march and their relief at finally escaping the horrors of the tunnel. Tan pondered on that and wondered where this tunnel was, he'd have to ask Alton about it. Added to that they muttered about the disappearance of a few of the corps who were normally with them. Boring stuff, he hoped Alton had been able to get more information than he had.

CHAPTER TWENTY

AUTUMN

She shifted her body so that her hands were hidden from sight as she slipped a dagger from its hiding place within the top of one of her boots. No matter what the outcome she was going to fight for the life of her pony.

It was easy to slice through the ropes that were binding her, and she wriggled her hands and wrists to let the blood flow through to them, readying for the moment she would need to jump up.

Her eyes tracked the executioner who had stopped to sharpen his knife on a whetstone and when he looked satisfied at his handiwork and began to head across towards his prey she leapt to her feet. At the same time Blackberry screamed angrily spinning around so that his hindquarters knocked his assailant to the ground and he gave a little buck to smash his hooves on the man's arm. Then out of nowhere a streak of fur crossed Autumn's eyeline and with a loud roar leapt onto the soldier. He didn't move again.

The leader shouted to his men that they were under attack as Autumn sprung onto his back pushing her knife into his shoulder. It made a horrible shushing sound as it sliced through the muscles. He was so surprised he fell to the ground moaning but then the grey ball of fur pounced on him and he was a goner, blood spurting from the wound where his neck had been bitten.

With a gust of wind, the dragon swept down from the sky landing perfectly in the small clearing snatching at the remaining soldiers one by one and tossing them high in the air.

The area was soon a bloody mess of bodies and bits of arms and legs.

Once she was sure that it was safe to do so, Autumn rushed across to Blackberry and buried her head in his neck.

"I thought… I really thought we had no hope! I couldn't bear to be without you!" she sobbed, relieved to find that the pony was unscathed.

Then remembering her manners, she looked across at the dragon who was delicately cleaning his talons.

She bowed her head to him, "Thank you, Shining Leaves! Thank you for saving my pony's life… and mine for that matter! You were amazing and I am so sorry I doubted you! But… who came to help you?"

She felt something touch her leg and looked down at the grey furry head hearing the purr that emitted from its whole body.

What was this creature? It looked like a big cat with huge paws but with the head and tail of a wolf.

Running her fingers along its body, she said, "Without you I do not think Blackberry would have survived, I thank you from the bottom of my heart!"

The dragon told her, "That is a wolf-cat and she knows Tan. He has been very worried about you."

A huge sigh came from her body. "So Tan is alright?"

"It would seem so. Alpha, is what he calls her. She sensed that you were in trouble and came as quickly as she could."

Autumn continued stroking the soft fur. The wolf-cat was a big animal, her head coming nearly up to Autumn's waist.

"I am in awe of you both!"

She was silent for a while as she listened to the purring from the animal and watched Shining Leaves trying to return himself to his usual state of perfection.

"Would... would you like me to reach that bit of mess on your shoulder for you? I could rub it with a leaf."

The dragon lowered himself to his stomach and inclined his head indicating that she could approach him. The scales that she touched felt strong but leathery under her fingers as she buffed at the various spots of dried blood marring his beautiful scales. He appeared to enjoy the attention and it wasn't long before he was his gleaming self again.

"Perfect!" she announced.

In the meantime, Alpha had laid down on her back and was squirming about in the dust.

"Shall I brush you too?"

The wolf-cat purred and stood up moving closer to the girl.

Everything from the bags was spread across the ground but eventually she found a brush and groomed Alpha in much the same way as she would have done to Blackberry, the wolf-cat groaning in pleasure.

"Now, don't you both look a picture?!" Autumn announced as she now turned herself to sorting out Blackberry.

It was soothing work making sure the pony was comfortable, and as she brushed a question popped up in her mind, "Leaf, could Alpha lead me to Tan?"

The dragon looked over at her before replying, "In theory, that would be possible but…"

An unknown but gentle voice from behind her joined in the conversation, "But in practice that would not be a sensible choice at all."

CHAPTER TWENTY-ONE

TAN

A strange feeling came over him as he stood in the small glade waiting for his Master to arrive. He shivered.

Alton strode into the clearing.

"Have you been through your stretches?" a nod was the answer. "Then, ready yourself!"

Before Tan could bat an eyelid, he was under attack, the librarian's staff flicking this way and that and catching him totally unawares.

"Concentrate!"

It was hard to do just that because part of his mind was still pondering over the oddness that he'd felt – what had caused it?

Before he knew it, he was flat on his back in the dirt.

"Now get up!" Alton shouted at him, "What is it that is distracting you?"

"I have this feeling that something is happening elsewhere, but I have no idea why."

"Well for now forget it and start blocking me!"

With a huge effort the lad began to spar, his own staff meeting that of his Master with a crash and sparks crackled in the air.

"See, your staff is beginning to work with you!" Alton wasn't out of breath at all moving smoothly and silently backwards and forwards. Tan on the other hand was, but at long last felt he was beginning to put up a good fight.

It was a relief to hear the words, "Rest." And Tan ran his hand down the length of the staff feeling it tremble beneath his fingers.

"You are right Sir, the staff recognises me."

"Considering it is only a short while since you cut and shaped it, believe me when I tell you that the bond between you will grow stronger and stronger. It is coming alive with your magic."

Tan took a sip out of the water bottle he had sensibly brought with him.

"We will be leaving this afternoon."

"What?!… But what about Autumn?"

"We have our own mission which has now become quite urgent so we cannot wait for her."

"But… but what is our mission, Sir?"

"Firstly, we need to make sure that Lord Nivers is aware of the coup that has taken place in Wick and that it is quite likely to escalate into his domain. He will have to prepare his troops or be taken by surprise."

Tan didn't know what to say, he was torn between his desire to please his Master and his worry about Autumn, but as he thought of her, he imagined he heard a loud purr in his head and his hand automatically went to the exact

84

spot on his cheek that Autumn had kissed all those days ago. He straightened up. What did that mean?!

"Are you alright, boy?"

"Well, Sir..." and he told him rather hesitantly about the purr that had just resounded through his head.

"Was the purr a soft, calming one?"

"Yes, it was almost as if I was stroking her."

"Then, trust me, that is likely the magic from the wolf-cat telling you all is well. Don't ask me how or why, some things remain a mystery. Now, perhaps you will concentrate and hear about a task I require you to perform."

As they walked back together at a good pace, Alton explained what Tan was to do.

* * *

Following the soldiers who'd been downing their pints the night before was quite easy because a couple of them had fallen asleep with their heads resting on one of the tables in the bar. Tan felt some sympathy for them having been in much the same position himself. When they staggered outside all he had to do was keep track of them from a distance. They were swaying about holding one another upright and had no sense to check if anyone was behind them.

There was guffawing when the soldiers stumbled into the camp site, and he took the opportunity to creep towards a decent sized tree and scramble up high into the branches where the leaves gave him good cover. He could hear the various conversations which were taking place as soon as the laughter had died down.

The captain in charge rallied the men, totally ignoring the two drunks.

"Take down the camp and ready yourselves to march to Wick! Those are our orders from above. As soon as we arrive, we will join another unit and be despatched to the castle at Hertle and we want to look the best we can. I am telling you this now because in the past we have always been a tight unit, watching each other's backs, which is essential in our line of work, and that needs to continue. No more carousing in bars," and he glared at the two latecomers, "we will need every bit of our energies to stay alive. I am sure that word will have already reached Hertle and it is likely to be a battle to the death for some soldiers! But, not us! We look after one another!"

The men shouted and clapped at the rousing speech.

"Get ready to march within the hour!" Then he turned to the laggards. "You two, come with me, I need a word!"

Tan watched the captain lead the men away from the camp, accompanied by two burly soldiers, one of them holding a leather whip. Then he heard what he thought could only be the sound of someone being thrashed soundly. When the soldiers returned the two drunks were white in the face, obviously in some pain. As they passed by Tan's hiding place he could see blood seeping through the backs of their jackets and he almost felt sorry for them.

Once he was sure that everyone was engrossed in breaking camp, he slithered down the tree trunk and set off at a jog back to the village to report to Alton.

CHAPTER TWENTY-TWO

AUTUMN

"Who are you, and what do you mean that would not be a sensible choice?" She stared at the pale-faced newcomer who was dressed totally in green, a longbow strapped across his body.

"Your friends are now on the move and unless you go back the way you came, which will mean running the risk of coming across more troops, you will need to take the route through the tunnel that the soldiers came through. In the tunnel there are dangers that you could not possibly imagine."

"How do you know where Tan and Alton are?" she asked, looking stunned, listening to the loud purring of the wolf-cat who was winding in and out of her legs.

"You will have to trust me on this."

The dragon broke his silence and added, "That is the truth for sure, my young friend and I will not be able to come with you through the tunnel, I can only wait at the other end of it for when you emerge. I have checked and there are only a few stragglers who are just approaching the other end, as we speak."

"If the tunnel is the quickest route, then that is what I must do! I will leave now."

The stranger looked deep into her eyes, "In that case you will die! Come with me and we will try and prepare you as best we can for the horrors you will have to face."

"But… but I don't know you at all!"

"You may not believe this, but your mother and I grew up together and she brought you to our village from time to time when you were very young."

Shining Leaves added, "I will accompany you on foot because the tree canopy is too dense above their village."

The wolf-cat purred even louder knocking at Autumn's knees with her huge paw as if to say, "Me too."

Even Blackberry gave her a nudge.

"Well, it seems I am outnumbered. Thank you, kind sir, I will accept your invitation. Can I ask what I should call you?"

"My name is Neldon, and I am the leader of the Fair Folk. Come, let us leave this dreadful place, it reeks of death. These were bad men, very bad indeed and I feel no remorse at their deaths, none at all!"

It was a strange procession, Neldon was in front, followed closely by Autumn, who felt like a grubby mess particularly as her usually tidy hair had come out of its plait. Blackberry was his usual gleaming self, the bags again holding the girl's spare clothing and other bits and pieces were attached to the saddle. Alpha was padding alongside and last of all came Shining Leaves.

Treading carefully down the path she wracked her brains trying hard to remember her mother speaking of the village deep in the woods. Nothing came to mind. She looked again at the wolf-cat and dragon who were now part of her entourage – she might not remember being brought to visit before, but she'd always remember this moment in time. Always.

The pathway widened as Neldon lead them into a village which was something out of the realm of dreams. The dwellings were part of the trees, steps going up inside wide tree trunks and when her eyes followed the trunks upwards what she saw was breathtaking. Walkways made of strands of what looked like ivy and treads of wood were suspended high above going from tree to tree. In the very centre of the area was an absolutely huge tree, the trunk being nearly the width of Autumn's small cottage and up high the leafy canopy let sunlight through which shone brightly onto small gardens. It was a beautiful and peaceful place.

Neldon gave a whistle and people dressed much like him began to appear on the wooden balconies linking the trees. They stared down at the strange array of visitors that followed the Fair Folk leader into the clearing. At the sight of the wolf-cat and the dragon one woman clapped loudly and before long the whole audience had joined in cheering and shouting in delight.

Suddenly a crowd of children ran out from the nearby trees and surrounded the dragon and the wolf-cat.

Autumn thought she had best check that this was acceptable to her companions, "Shining Leaves, I believe they would like to touch you and Alpha, is that allowed?"

The dragon preened looking so proud and gave a small nod of his beautiful head. The wolf-cat lay down as if waiting to be petted.

"They are happy for you to touch them, but it might be even better if in a while you could bring Shining Leaves some acorns – they are his favourite snack!" Autumn announced and before she knew it there were children of all ages stroking the beasts. One rather brave boy was struggling to get up on Leaf's back. The girl bit her tongue, worrying that the dragon would be angry but he lowered himself to the ground, much as Alpha had done, revelling in the attention.

"Come!" Neldon gestured to Autumn, "Let us get you cleaned up and find you a place to stay. Then we will feast!"

* * *

Autumn stretched out on the comfortable pallet she'd been given, looking up at the roof over her head – it was made of strands of beautifully plaited circles of ivy that made swirls above her. As with everything in this village, it seemed to be made with a lot of care and she sighed contentedly. For the first time since she'd left her home, she felt safe.

CHAPTER TWENTY-THREE

TAN

They had trekked long into the night using the stars to guide them. Tan walked beside his Master and listened intently to a lesson on the sky above them.

"If you learn where the stars are in the night sky you will never get lost," Alton told him.

"How much further is it to the castle?"

"We stop soon to camp a little way outside of its boundaries. Early tomorrow morning we will make our entrance because it will be better to do so after a good night's rest. I have no idea what we will have to face, it may be as normal or there could be trouble so we will need to be prepared for whatever comes our way."

They were up when the sun rose heading towards their destination. Tan had slept well that night and felt good – his staff tingling in his hands.

"Use it as a walking stick and pretend to hobble and

need it to support you – we do not want to be challenged and for them to try and take it from you."

"Yes, Sir."

Crossing the moat which surrounded the castle, they were stopped by soldiers at the main gate.

"Who goes there?"

"It is I, Alton, the librarian, here to see Lord Nivers. He is expecting me!"

The soldier peered back and then turned to check with his partner if they could be let through.

"I'm sure a librarian will not offer any problems for the Lord," they agreed. "But who is this accompanying you?"

"That is my apprentice, Tancred. He has hurt his foot and needs to use the stick for the time being. Hopefully, it will soon be mended because he is of little use to me being injured! Stupid boy wasn't looking where he was going and tripped in a rabbit hole."

Tan dipped his head as if he was ashamed, while trying hard not to laugh.

"You may pass. We will send a runner to let the Lord know of your arrival."

"Thank you, kind sir."

The pair continued through in silence, Tan making a big thing of having to lean on his staff.

His Master muttered, "That was strange, I did not know either of those men and in the past the same gatekeepers have always rotated on duty. What's more, did you notice the colours they were wearing?"

"It was red and green, Master."

"Quite so, not the uniform of Lord Nivers. Be on your guard boy, we may be facing some danger here."

After stopping at the stables and making sure the mule was well looked after they went straight to a small room next to the library. Tan shivered, it was colder in here than outside. A single bed was in one corner and a desk in another. Two comfortable looking armchairs faced the fireplace where a fire was built ready to be lit. His Master waved his hand and soon flames licked upwards emitting welcome heat into the room.

"I will ask them to bring a pallet for you to sleep on, I have never brought anyone with me before so they would not have expected you. Let's stow our goods in that cupboard and go down to the main hall. I would imagine there will be a good many people having breakfast, which in the past has always been a substantial one. It is possible the Lord will be there too. Make sure you keep your staff with you at all times, you may need it!"

"Sir!"

Tan concentrated on the route to the main hall, taking note of any staircases which led down from the main walkway. A maid came up one such staircase carrying a tray of lovely smelling warm bread and a dish of bacon, so Tan guessed that must be the way to the kitchens.

When they entered the hall he made a big show of leaning on his staff and limping as if he were in great pain.

His Master stopped just inside the doorway and surveyed the room briefly before continuing to the large table that was on a plinth making it a little higher than the other trestles and benches that were placed throughout the room.

"This way, boy! Keep up!" he barked at his apprentice.

As they neared the platform, Alton called out, "Lord Nivers, how good to see you! I do apologise for the delay in my arrival, but I am delighted to be with you now!"

There were two men seated at the table and Tan assumed the one who was dressed in rather expensive looking and bright garb in red and green was Lord Nivers. He tried not to show his surprise when the other man looked up at them.

"Who... who are you?" his voice quavered.

His richly dressed companion bent his head and said, "That is Alton, the librarian. You remember, you invited him to look for some information in the library?"

"Yes... yes, of course," was the answer.

Tan was shocked, the Lord's eyes were unfocussed almost as if he was in a trance.

The other man addressed Alton, "His Lordship has been unwell for a while, so I have been assisting him with the running of the estate. My name is Dintern."

Alton bowed his head, "I am pleased to meet you Lord Dintern. It is good that there is someone to help Lord Nivers, but what of his wife, is she unable to do so?"

A very brief flash of annoyance crossed Dintern's face before he smoothed it over, all smiles.

"I'm not a Lord, I'm afraid, but Lady Nivers has also been somewhat indisposed and has had to keep to her suite of late. Have you visited your own room?"

"Yes, thank you and we have left our belongings there. I have lit the fire but would be very grateful if another bed could be brought there for my apprentice, such that he is!" Alton sneered. "He has been foolish enough to injure his foot and that is the reason our journey here has taken so long."

After a hearty breakfast of crispy bacon, eggs and fried potatoes Alton led Tan back to their room where they were pleased to find another bed had been placed along one of the walls.

Alton opened the cupboard and nodded, "Of course! Although they have tried to do it discreetly, our belongings have been searched. It is as well we have come here because matters are not right!"

CHAPTER TWENTY-FOUR
AUTUMN

The view from the pinnacle of the enormous tree was breath-taking! She could see for miles and miles.

"There, in the distance you can see the Wick castle, and over that way is the castle belonging to Lord Nivers. And there is Hertle, to the far right," Autumn's companion told her.

She had woken feeling totally refreshed and very hungry and as soon as she emerged from the room she had been allocated in the tree canopy, a girl had greeted her. It seemed she had been waiting for Autumn to wake.

"I wanted to let you sleep as long as possible," were her first words, "I am Lindy and Neldon asked me to look after you."

"How kind."

They breakfasted on fruit, cheese and bread and then visited Blackberry to check he was alright. He was quite content, so when Lindy offered to show her the view from the heights she had been more than happy to accept.

Autumn was a little out of breath by the time they had climbed the circular staircase which rose up and up inside the huge tree that heralded the centre of the compound, but it was certainly worth it when they reached the very top.

"Wow! Amazing!"

Below them stretched a canopy of leaves showing just how the huge tree dwarfed the others in the dark forest. The leaves below her swished gently in the light breeze and the odd bird screeched as it flew across the sky.

"I have never seen anything quite so beautiful before!" she breathed, "What's more I can now see where the different castles are in relation to one another. Why I ever thought they were quite near to one another shows how wrong I was."

Lindy smiled, seeming pleased with the reaction she'd received from Autumn.

"When you're ready, I'll show you the rest of the village and introduce you to some of the others and then, after lunch Neldon will have time to talk to you. I'm sure you have lots of questions and he is best placed to answer them. He is a mine of information!" the girl sounded quite in awe of the chief of the Fair Folk.

By the time they had finished their tour Autumn's head was reeling. So many names to remember. What had amused her was when she saw how Shining Leaves was enjoying the attention he was receiving. Of Alpha there was no sign, but Lindy had told her that the wolf-cat was about somewhere for sure.

Lunch took place in Lindy's parents' home where she was welcomed with open arms. It was a cold but colourful repast consisting of many different salads and nuts and what surprised Autumn, cold chicken.

"I didn't notice any chickens running about, where are they kept?"

"All of our animals and hens are housed in a compound a stone's throw away," Lindy's mum explained. "We used to keep them down below near the centre of our village, but it became a huge task keeping the smell down – it ponged so much. Where they are now means that twice a day someone is tasked with mucking out the area and the waste moved to a pile just outside the animal compound where it is used to make manure for the vegetable plots and fruit trees."

"That's what we used to do in our village," Autumn exclaimed. "I'd have to wheelbarrow Blackberry's droppings to a communal muck heap, and then in the autumn everyone would get a share of the compost for the vegetable patches." Just talking about home made her eyes well and she ducked her head so that no-one would notice.

Lindy had sharp vision though and rested a comforting hand on Autumn's arm, "Don't worry, you'll see it again!"

The auburn-haired girl then thought back to what Lindy's mum had just said. "But don't fruit trees need light and sunshine to produce fruit?"

Her daughter just smiled as she replied, "I'll show you around our whole estate either today or tomorrow, depending on how much time we have, and you'll soon see."

Autumn felt very relaxed later as they strolled to where Neldon was expecting her to join him. The ivy roped walkway swayed gently in the breeze as they headed towards one of what appeared to be an older residence. It was a little larger than some of the newer ones and set right out at the edge of the high village.

Knocking on the doorframe her companion called out, "It is I, Lindy!"

"Come in then, come in! You took your time girl I've been waiting for you to bring me my guest!"

A woman was rocking backwards and forwards in a chair made out of the same dark wood as the walls. Neldon was beside her, smiling a welcome to them.

The room felt strangely familiar.

"Well, come closer girl! My old eyes are not what they were and I want to take a look at you!"

Autumn obeyed, slowly and when she was immediately in front of the chair, she sank to her haunches to enable the occupant of the rocking chair to see her more clearly. The rheumy eyes peered across at her and a very wrinkled hand stretched towards her and stroked her arm gently.

"You look just like your mother did at your age."

"How… how could you know that?" Autumn couldn't take her eyes off of the woman. "You… you look like someone I should know!" was all she could think to say.

She nearly toppled over when the answer came back at her, "Well, girl, so I should, I am your grandmother!"

CHAPTER TWENTY-FIVE

TAN

Tan was not quite sure how he was going to carry out his instructions, but Alton had been insistent that he would find a way. Held gently in his left hand was a tiny pellet – the other hand was grasping the staff firmly as he hobbled towards the head table in the refectory. It was a huge effort not to turn his head to look at his Master who was standing close to the big fireplace and was regaling Dintern and his companion with tales of their journey to the castle. Every now and then they would guffaw loudly and look across at Tan which made him think that he, himself, was probably the butt of their jokes.

He pretended to head towards them and not to his real target, Lord Nivers. The Lord was rather feebly trying to spoon some soup into his mouth and a lot of it dribbled down his chin onto his clothing, much as if he was a baby.

As Tan neared the table, he moved the small pellet so that it rested between his thumb and forefinger. The librarian had assured him that the coating on the pill would protect him if his hands sweated. Stumbling as if his foot had given way he knocked into his Lordship's shoulder making the soup bowl wobble precariously and splashing yet more of its contents over the Lord's clothing. With sleight of hand, he dropped the tablet into the soup before letting himself crash to the floor. Tan thought he could hear the hiss of the liquid as the pellet was absorbed. Lord Nivers seemed almost unaware of the ruckus that had been caused continuing to spoon soup rather waveringly to his mouth again and again.

"I am so sorry, my Lord!" he said breathlessly to his Lordship as he dragged himself to his feet.

Loud footsteps came up behind him and Alton spun him around shouting loudly, "You, useless, clumsy boy! Look what you have done to Lord Nivers' clothing! How on earth could I have picked such a stupid lad as my apprentice?!" He pulled on Tan's ear and told him to go back to their room and wait for him. "No... don't say another word! Just go!"

Obediently he clasped his staff and began to stagger back in the direction of the way they had come. He could hear Dintern sniggering nastily as if he was enjoying the spectacle of a servant being told off, the man's eyes tracked Tan all the way not noticing Alton whispering quietly in Lord Nivers' ear.

"Job done!" he thought to himself, trying not to let pride show on his face.

As he turned the corner, he could hear his Master offering to accompany Lord Nivers to his room to help him change his tunic, "Because that idiot of a boy has managed

101

to soak you and that must be so very uncomfortable for you!"

Tan slowed his steps even more – the plan was actually that the apprentice would join them in Lord Nivers' rooms but, he had no idea how to get there so was going to need to follow them, so long as Dintern or his soldiers didn't tag along.

Alton's voice was loud enough for all to hear as he came along the stone corridor and Tan, checked no-one was about before he slipped into a shadowy dark alcove. His Master and the Lord ambled slowly past him.

Tan stayed put… it was essential that he wasn't seen and when he was positive there was no-one keeping an eye on Alton and the Lord he moved out of his hideaway and sped off in pursuit. It was only a few moments before he saw Alton hesitating briefly to make sure his apprentice was within sight.

It was a relief to finally reach the safety of Lord Nivers' rooms where Alton was waiting for him and closed the door quietly behind him.

"Stay behind this door please, Tan so that if anyone does enter without knocking you will not be on view. Lord Nivers and I will be just over here." He turned to the Lord. "Sir, you seem to be coming back to us."

"I feel as if I am coming out of a deep fog. What has happened to me?"

Alton looked serious as he explained, "Well, my Lord, my guess is that you have been poisoned in some way or other. My apprentice has done a superb job of slipping the very fast acting antidote that I gave him into your soup and fortunately you continued supping it. Very soon you should be back to your old self… but what shall we do to keep you safe? Do you have any trusted men here in the castle, because it seems to me that all of the soldiers I have seen today have been wearing the colours of Dintern."

Tan could see from where he was standing the amazing change in the Lord's features taking place as his gaze lost its haziness.

"That man! I knew he was trouble when he arrived but there wasn't much I could do about it. I am so glad my dear Alton that you continued your journey here safely," he stopped as he considered the options ahead of them. "My guess is that my own men will be in the local tavern, "The Blue Buck", but how we can get a message to them I know not. It is also quite likely that Dintern will send one of his minions to check on me if I do not return to the refectory."

"Never fear my Lord. I will send my apprentice to him with a message that as you seem so tired, I have assisted you to your bed. Tan, can I entrust you to do that? Beware though, that nasty man is quite likely to hurt you if he can."

Tan nodded his agreement not too concerned because his body was still recovering from sparing with his mentor the day before.

"While you are gone, Lord Nivers and I will put our heads together and try and come up with a plan going forwards."

* * *

As it happened, his Master was quite correct – Dintern certainly enjoyed slapping Tan about and when the man had finished showing off in front of his cronies Tan didn't have to pretend to hobble this time, his leg hurt where he'd been kicked.

Once out of sight, he muttered to himself, "I will get you back for that beating, you old pig! That's a promise!"

CHAPTER TWENTY-SIX

AUTUMN

Shock held her totally still for a moment until she managed to say quietly, "I never knew that I had a grandmother, but I guess I didn't actually ask the question."

The old woman's hair was largely grey but there was a sprinkling of copper at the edges, the same as Autumn's hair.

"So... so I did come here when I was very young? Neldon said I had."

"Yes, your mother used to bring you to visit me from time to time. She left our community after she met your father. They were married here, under the trees and then went to live at the forge in Wick."

"They are still very happy together and I love them very much... but I am so worried about how they are faring now that Lord Travers' brother has ousted him and taken over the castle."

"Do not fret, my dear," her grandmother told her. "We have been keeping an eye from afar. Your father has been allowed to return to the forge where he is kept fully busy making sure the soldiers' horses are well shod and ready for their next foray into battle. Your mother is back in the school teaching. They are under guard the whole time so there is no question of them escaping, but they are well looked after, mainly because they are both necessary to the new Lord." Autumn gave a sigh of relief.

"Thank goodness for that!"

"Your father made it quite clear that he would not work if a hair on your mother's head was touched. He is a good man, and he has also done his best to protect the other villagers, but that has not been so easy. If anyone has an essential trade they are allowed to work in the village, but if not, they are kept locked up in the castle."

Autumn felt as if a weight had been lifted from her to hear her parents were alive and alright, but she felt concern for the others, after all they were a very small and close knit community always looking out for one another.

"Do you know anything about Tan's mother, sister and brother?"

"I'm afraid not, my dear, but we are not aware of anyone being put to death."

Her grandmother held out her arms and the girl flung herself into them – a cuddle was just what she needed right now, and one from a family member was the best.

It was Neldon's voice that broke the embrace.

"Autumn, you have arrived here with a dragon and a wolf-cat and that is something very special. How did that come about?"

"Well… it was actually Tan who met Shining Leaves first…" and she launched into the tale of everything that had taken place before disaster had hit the village.

"As I told you, I really do need to catch up with Tan and Alton so that we can work out how to save the Lord and the villagers."

"Hmm… that is very noble of you my dear, particularly as you have no arms training."

"But I am pretty good with a bow and arrow!" she retorted.

Her grandmother interrupted. "I should think so too! That is something that us Fair Folk are renowned for. Neldon, take her to the range and let her prove herself to you."

* * *

The rest of the afternoon was spent in an area a short distance from the village. Autumn was surprised to see targets set up at different distances, much as she had done for herself at home. She took Blackberry with her just to give him a change of scenery and Alpha appeared from out of nowhere, purring loudly, her big paws padding along next to the pony.

Neldon was silent on their walk back, waiting patiently while she settled Blackberry down and gave him his evening feed before they returned to her grandmother's cottage. The wolf-cat curled up just outside the doorway in the walkway looking quite content. Lindy was sitting on a small stool by the rocking chair, winding wool and she gave Autumn a quick smile.

"Well, man! How was she?"

Neldon cleared his throat looking very serious before he replied, "She is one of the best I have ever seen! I think she would beat many of our own archers, and to my great surprise she can also shoot accurately from horseback!"

"If you remember, her mother was equally as good."

"That I do."

Autumn's cheeks reddened at the praise and she looked down at her feet.

"Sit, my dear. Let us eat together. Lindy has brought food for us all to share," the old woman said.

It was another fun meal, Lindy made them all laugh as she told them how the children had brought Shining Leaves a pile of acorns and were throwing them one by one for him to snatch out of the air. They were also using him as a slide.

"But if he didn't like it, he would soon let them know, I'm sure," she added.

As they ate Autumn glowed with pleasure when she was asked if she would like to move into her grandmother's home.

"There is a spare room here which was your mothers, and it would give us a short time to get to know one another before you set off on your journey."

"I would love to! Thank you!"

The night passed swiftly, and Autumn was up early the next morning feeling totally refreshed and relaxed. She was sure that her bed still smelled of her mother and she felt enveloped in love.

It had been decided that Autumn should learn how to protect herself – a bow and arrow would not suffice.

"I appreciate that your father has taught you some defensive moves, but we need to go further than that," Neldon told her.

He asked Lindy to summon another member of the Fair Folk to the arena where the targets were.

As they waited, the girl asked, "Why are you called Fair Folk? Am I also Fair Folk?"

"Many years ago, at the beginning of some war a few of our ancestors moved into the forest because they believed they would be safer there, hidden amongst the trees. When they emerged to begin trading with the people who lived in the area it was obvious that their skins were much lighter than those who lived under the sun. Someone nicknamed them Fair Folk, and that name has stuck," he hesitated for a moment. "Your mother was one of the Fair Folk but since she has left the protection of the tree canopy she is not really thought of as one and neither can you be."

Autumn nodded, that made good sense to her.

"For all that," Neldon added, "we will protect you as one of our own."

Her eyes watered at the kindness in his voice.

"Th… thank you!" was all she could manage to say, but at that moment the bushes rustled announcing the arrival of a woman totally clad in green.

"Well met, Neldon!" she greeted him as she bowed her head slightly.

"And you, Allina!"

The woman turned to look Autumn up and down as if assessing her before she nodded, as if approving what she had seen.

"Allina, this is Autumn who I have told you about and Autumn, this is Allina, one of our most skilled warriors. She trains all of us in the art of fighting just in case we should need protection. It is not something we Fair Folk are known for, but then that has the surprise factor if it should ever be required. She is the best! I will leave you two together."

Before she knew it Autumn was moving her body this way and that which had she but known it, almost mirrored those that her friend, Tan now performed.

CHAPTER TWENTY-SEVEN

TAN

Tan had to force his body to obey him to carry out the next part of his instructions. He ached all over and his gait was very unsteady.

Returning to where a set of armour was standing in a shadowy corner just outside their room, he retrieved the staff that was held in its stiff hand. It trembled at his touch. He had deemed it best to leave the staff behind if he was going to get a beating from Dintern because he had this odd sense that the staff wouldn't have stood for its master being pummelled to the ground. He put the walking stick which he'd found in a corner of their room into the armoured fist in its place.

As soon as he had the staff in his hand, he felt kind of renewed.

"This magic stuff is rather weird," he thought.

He'd been told to follow the corridor to the very end and then go down the stairs which lead to the kitchens.

Keeping to the shadows as much as possible, checking behind him every now and then to make sure he wasn't being followed, he began the descent into the depths of the servants' area.

The aromas circulating in the room were so fabulous, they made him drool. The cook, though intent on giving instructions to one of the maids, noticed him.

"You lad!"

"Yes, ma'am?" he answered politely.

"I hear you took a beating… very unfair in my view. Would you like some food before you get on your way? I won't ask where you're off to."

His stomach rumbled as he replied, "A quick snack would be amazing, if that's possible." He wasn't at all sure when he would next be able to eat and he had time while he waited for dusk to fall before making his way to his next destination.

With the rattle of a big spoon the woman passed a bowl of stew to the girl with her. The maid gave him a shy smile as she put it down before him, along with a big piece of crusty bread.

He demolished it in a very short time.

"Thank you, that was absolutely delicious!"

"You are welcome," the cook said. "Whenever you need food, don't hesitate to come down here – any of us will make sure you and your Master are fed, and well at that!"

"You are so very kind, that is really good to know."

The woman bent her head to his ear and whispered, "We do not like the new broom which is trying to take over! None of us in the servants' quarters do but be aware we do have one or two new members of staff who have been foisted on us and they are not loyal to the old Lord."

"Is there any way I can tell which ones they are?" he asked quietly.

"Their uniforms will be crisp and new, but look at their footwear particularly, they wear black soldier's boots."

"That is so very helpful, thank you. I will avoid them if I possibly can. Now, I had better be on my way although I will probably come back through the kitchens on my return if that is alright?"

"That is fine, but Millie here can show you another less known entrance to the servants' quarters. Millie! Please show this young man the other doorway please."

The girl bobbed her agreement and then waved at Tan to follow her.

She took him through the pantry where, tucked at the very end, there was a wooden doorway which couldn't be seen until one reached it.

"Go through here," she told him quietly, "and it will lead you to the side of the courtyard around the corner to the main servants' entrance. The door is never locked and the servants, barring the newer ones, use it when they are out later than they should be."

"Thank you, Millie! I appreciate it! Keep safe!" and he gave a small bow ending with a flourish of his hand, which made her giggle.

There were a few worn stone steps leading to a wooden door which he cracked open to survey the scene in front of him. The courtyard was deserted, but just as he was about to step outside, he spotted someone moving. Pressing himself against the wall he watched the man, or was it a woman? He couldn't be sure as they were wearing a dark cloak with a hood up.

Staying very still he watched another shadowy person crossing the courtyard. He could tell from the way they walked that they were either a soldier or someone wearing soldier's boots.

Their voices were very quiet and muffled. He gripped his staff tightly and was stunned to find his hearing was much clearer as a result. Magic at work again!

"Did you follow the boy?"

"I lost him near the room he shares with the librarian," a woman's voice answered.

"Idiot!" and Tan heard a loud slap. "We sent you because he wouldn't notice or worry about someone dressed as a serving girl! We need to find him, and soon or else there will be hell to pay. We have to keep tabs on the boy and his Master."

"The Master is still in with his Lordship, but when I looked in on them his Lordship was asleep on the bed and Alton was nodding in an armchair in front of the fire. He must have been tired after his journey."

"Good! Now, off you go and search for the boy. Did you check their room again?"

"I will do so now, sir," she answered saluting before turning on her heels.

She crossed the courtyard heading towards the main servants' doorway and Tan got a whiff of perfume – not something a serving girl would wear. He inhaled quietly making sure he would remember the next time he smelled it.

Waiting for quite a few minutes before he moved was frustrating, – he wanted to get on with his allotted task.

114

CHAPTER TWENTY-EIGHT

AUTUMN

The campfire was blazing, sparks flying upwards, as musicians played their instruments near the huge old tree. Shining Leaves was basking nearby, enjoying the heat that was coming towards him. Every now and then his reptilian eyelids would lift and he would survey the dancers cavorting in front of him.

"How can you have a big fire like this in the middle of the forest?" Autumn asked her grandmother.

"We have to place it exactly where it is now, and the heat and flames are drawn up towards the gap in the tree canopy high above. I have to admit, it took a few trial efforts before we found the right place for it." Her foot was tapping in time with the music.

A pair of legs stopped in front of Autumn. They were clad in what looked like a soft green fabric.

"Would the young lady care to dance?" a gentle voice enquired.

The girl looked up at the young man who was speaking to her but before she could answer, her grandmother urged her to join him.

"Have some fun!" she told her. "I wish my old bones would allow me to dance, but they are past their prime."

Autumn rather reluctantly rose to her feet, looking a bit embarrassed.

"I… I am not used to dancing and probably have two left feet." She told her prospective partner.

He laughed, "Makes it all the more enjoyable. Relax, come with me. My name is Ronan and I know you are Autumn – what better name for someone with your hair colour!"

Out of the corner of her eye the girl saw Alpha prowl into the edge of the clearing and pace backwards and forwards as if on watch.

"Your wolf-cat is beautiful, much like her owner!" Ronan told her.

Autumn, feeling very uncomfortable at the praise managed to tell him, "The wolf-cat does not belong to me – she is a wild beast who I have only just come across."

"Well, you should consider yourself honoured, they are not known for forming a bond with a human. For that matter, neither are dragons!"

Shining Leaves must have heard himself being talked about because he raised his head and watched the two of them as they began a slow circuit of the people dancing near to the fire. As the music quickened so did their footsteps and by the end of the tune, Autumn was laughing and quite out of breath.

"Thank you, kind sir! That was most enjoyable!"

"Ronan!" a nearby voice called, "I've been looking for you! You promised me a dance!"

"I did that," he told Lindy and bowed to Autumn, before returning her to her grandmother's side.

That one dance seemed to release the shyness of the other young males and soon Autumn found herself dancing one reel and then another with a variety of different partners. She noticed that Lindy kept Ronan mostly to herself.

"So that is how the land lies," she thought smiling. "She has no worries from me. I wonder what Tan would make of all of this?"

* * *

With the morning came another bout of fighting skills from Allina. Some of the moves were quite difficult to perform but she was told that with practice they would come to her naturally. The hardest to take in were the ones which were to enable her to repel an attacker at close quarters, something that would have been useful when the soldiers had caught her.

"No! You don't need to use strength to win, just stealth!" the warrior told her. "Take them by surprise."

It was almost overwhelming trying to remember the move where if caught from behind she would smash the back of her head into the bridge of her attacker's nose. Or if face on she had to push her fingers up the other's nostrils, which Autumn found particularly gross.

It was very repetitive training – again and again Allina came at her from behind until it was an automatic move for Autumn to fling her head backwards.

"Muscle memory," the woman told her as they finally came to rest.

"But what of my daggers?" the girl asked her teacher.

"You might not have the freedom to reach your weapons, but if you do, I will show you how to use them. We are having to cover so much in such a short time to enable you to leave here before the bad weather comes and looking at the clouds that are gathering above the mountain, that will be much sooner than we would really like."

Alpha, who had been watching them closely as she licked her huge paws clean growled as if in agreement.

The afternoon was spent with Neldon who was to tutor her in how to deal with the many unusual dangers that she might come across in the tunnel.

"It is not a place to linger," he told her. "Some of the inhabitants are able to use magic. I know not where they came from, but believe me, they are not to be trifled with and even I, would fear them. I am not at all happy about you using that route but you seem determined to do so, and it is the quickest."

"But how did the soldiers get through unscathed?"

"What makes you think that some were not lost in the tunnel? After all there were so many of them and they were a raggedly bunch with no order amongst them."

That made Autumn think because he was quite right there was no way to know if any of the men had been taken by the beasts that lived in the darkness.

He used a stick to draw in the earth some of the hideous creatures that made Autumn shudder, particularly when she saw the poisonous spiders, which he said were the size of a pony and if they caught you with their pincers, you would be stunned. Then there were large snakelike worms with bulbous eyes which could travel silently at a great speed and catch one unawares. The list was quite a long one and Autumn needed to remember how to deal with each and every one, because some could be dealt with using a sword, others the bow and arrow and then there were those where it was best just to run as fast as possible.

Alpha kept close during the lesson, she seemed to understand that these creatures were something different to what she was used to. Every now and then Shining Leaves would also add his voice to what was being said. He had come across some of these enemies himself and had found that snorting fire was a great deterrent.

"Yes," agreed Neldon. "You will need flaming torches to light your way and you should be ready to use them to defend yourself, should you need to."

CHAPTER TWENTY-NINE

TAN

The warmth from the logs blazing in the huge fireplace hit Tan in the face when he entered the tavern. He stopped in the doorway trying to spot the man that he had been sent to find. Everyone in the room was wearing part of a uniform, but they all looked rather dishevelled.

Tan's eyes tracked each and every one of them before he strode forward towards the bar and his target. He'd hidden his staff in a pile of straw in the stables by the tavern considering it better if he didn't look as if he was armed. Using it as a crutch was also not appealing to him as that would make him seem weak. The men inside were either talking quietly or playing cards as they supped their tankards of ale.

The lad leant up against the bar as he tried to catch the eye of the barkeep.

"You'll have to wait your turn," the big man who was resting his elbow on the top of the bar told him.

"I will sir, never fear, I know my place." Tan turned his face to look the soldier beside him straight in the eyes, "Would you be Captain Smithers by any chance?"

"And who would be asking?"

Lowering his voice Tan replied, "I have been sent by his Lordship to find you – he gave me this which has his seal on it so that you would know to trust me," and he thrust a small piece of parchment over discreetly.

He could feel the man looking him up and down in surprise.

"And, why would the Lord send one such as you?"

"My name is Tancred, and I am apprenticed to the librarian, Alton. Alton is with Lord Nivers as we speak."

"Let me buy you an ale and we can talk. Tell me all that you know." It seemed there was no waiting in turn for the captain because two ales were thumped in front of him immediately he called for them.

* * *

Tan was happy to retrieve his staff before resuming his hobbling gait as he wended his way back to the castle. He could sense the captain wasn't too far behind him keeping to the shadows thrown by the buildings they passed by.

As he neared the castle wall, the apprentice paused in a dark corner and waited as he made sure that no-one other than the captain was nearby. A rustle of a cloak let him know that Captain Smithers had joined him, and they stood together, both alert to any movements around them.

Nothing.

"Follow me, sir! We are heading over just around the corner to the main servants' entrance."

They passed quietly through the kitchen, the cook so intent on stirring something that smelled delicious on the range that she didn't notice them slipping through. Fortunately, she was on her own.

"I take it you know the way to the Lord's rooms?"

"Yes, of course," the soldier replied.

"In that case when you get to the top of the steps please wait for a few minutes and I will draw off the watchers that will be nearby. Please ignore the fracus that is sure to take place and once it seems safe to do so, enter as quickly as possible. I will follow as soon as I am able."

The lad made a big show of limping down the corridor, although he did make a speedy stop by the suit of armour to switch his staff for the wooden stick. When he emerged from the shadowy alcove, he heard a snigger and before he had time to brace himself was knocked to the ground and a shiny boot kicked him in the ribs.

"Where have you been, boy!" a fierce voice came from above him.

"I went to the kitchens to get some food," he quavered. "and am now am going to… to my room, is that a problem?"

Another person with a lighter voice joined the conversation.

"Shall we give him a beating?"

"Best not, we don't want to upset the librarian, I've heard our new Lord has a job for him."

There was a whistle of air as his assailant slapped Tan hard across the face, before grabbing his arm and shoving him against the wall.

"Don't say a word to your Master about our meeting, or worse things will happen to you!" the man said menacingly and with a sneer the pair sauntered off along the corridor heading towards the main hall. Tan took a deep breath and then staggered towards his room and made a big show of opening the door and going inside.

"Another pair that I must remember that I owe! The list is growing!" he muttered before cracking open the door and peering out. They'd gone.

* * *

It was good to be back with his Master, a small glass of brandy in his hand. "It will help numb the pain of the beatings you have had to go through!" he was told. He'd never drunk a spirit before and found he needed to sip it because it burned his mouth.

Alton laughed kindly when he saw the grimace on the lad's face, "Don't worry, it's an acquired taste, consider it medicinal." Then he looked serious, "So we are all in agreement, there is someone else pulling the strings of the so-called new Lords?"

"Yes, but who?"

Frowning, the librarian answered, "In many of the books I have read over the years, it was predicted that Malvic would return!"

The Lord and Captain looked shocked, but it was Tan who said, "But, I thought that was just someone that had been made up to scare us children into behaving ourselves!"

"Oh no, my boy, believe me, he was real!"

CHAPTER THIRTY

AUTUMN

The tunnel entrance looked very unwelcoming as Autumn peered into its dark depths. Shivering she put her hand on Blackberry's neck as he stood stoically next to her.

Neldon nodded in understanding.

"I wish I could come with you but, it is not possible. As leader, I must gather the different factions of the Fair Folk to ready them for whatever may be coming, but…" and he looked behind him as Lindy stepped out of the nearby trees, she had a pack on her back and a sword at her waist. A longbow was across her shoulders.

"I will be accompanying you!" she announced and then surprise passed across Neldon's face as another joined them. Ronan.

"I too, am coming along."

"No! That is too much to ask!" Autumn stuttered in amazement.

"But you did not ask, and we both insist! Do not deny us the chance for us to prove ourselves, not just to you, but to the Fair Folk too!"

Alpha wound herself around the girl's legs as if to remind her that she too, would be with them.

"Well… thank you! That is… very kind! I must admit the company would be welcome, but what if you are killed or maimed by what we have to face."

Lindy touched her shoulder, "Of that we are aware, but we have made our decision – both of us!"

A whoosh of air announced the arrival of Shining Leaves as he landed perfectly in the small space next to her.

"I will walk with you until the tunnel narrows, but remember, you will have to gather lots of acorns when you reach the other end!" and his voice rumbled as if he was laughing.

A tear trickled down her cheek, she was overwhelmed at the support that they were giving her. She had to admit, it had been very daunting to think of going into the unknown on her own with only Blackberry and Alpha to accompany her. She brushed the wetness aside quickly, not wishing to show any fear.

"Thank you from the depths of my heart! I must say it is cheering to know that I will have you with me."

With a last farewell to Neldon, the company moved forward, Autumn at the head holding aloft a flaming torch. They had six of these between them in readiness to fend off the dangers that were ahead of them.

Autumn stroked the longbow that was over her shoulder and felt it sing at her touch, it had been a surprise gift from her grandmother. It was beautiful.

125

"This belonged to my mother before me and she was as skilled as you with her bow and arrow," she had told the girl. "Your mother had no need of it because she was leaving with your father but, believe me somehow it will help you in your quest, how, I do not know but it has magic imbued in it and it reacts to each of its owners in a different manner."

The longbow had shuddered under her fingers, its colour turning silver.

"It's… it's amazing! But you cannot give this to me!"

"I can, and I will. I can sense that it was meant for you so please take it, but before you leave you must practice using it at the range because it would be folly not to do so."

Autumn had spent the previous afternoon doing just that, and the longbow had performed astoundingly well. She had thought her own bow and arrow had been good but this one was in a different realm altogether. It was as if the longbow could sense what she needed to do and met every single target she aimed at bang on. When she'd returned full of the joys of spring to tell her grandmother all about it, the woman had just smiled at her as if to say, "I told you so!"

She fingered the final gift she had received, this time from Neldon.

"I know you have a good cloak of your own, but you will find this one easier to wear with the longbow across your back." It was made of a lightweight green material and had a hood which she could pull over her head and face to help her hide if necessary. Neldon had assured her that it was totally waterproof. Looking over at her pony she'd been thrilled to see that he too, had received such a gift which covered his haunches.

One of the young girls who had accompanied Neldon patted the pony smiling, "We love Blackberry, and this will keep him dry, even when he is getting hot and sweaty."

The pony had nickered and given the girl a gentle nudge as if to say, "Thank you!"

The tunnel was cold inside… very cold and Autumn shivered, really wanting just to run back out into the gentle sunshine.

"No!" she told herself, "You are meant to face whatever foes will come before us… you are now a leader! Remember that!" and she straightened her shoulders and lifted her head high.

The wolf-cat padded quietly along beside her, with Blackberry following on just behind. He needed no lead rope and it showed just how much he loved his owner that he had entered the tunnel without hesitation.

Ronan and Cindy walked side by side, their gaze focussing on what was ahead and the dragon could be heard snuffling at the rear. His talons rasping loudly against the stony floor and every now and then he would snort. He was not a quiet companion in such a small space by any amount of imagination. They were surrounded by a rather musty but unpleasant smell.

After a couple of hours their leader could see that the tunnel was narrowing bringing her to a halt.

"I believe this is where we have to leave you, my wonderful friend, Shining Leaves!"

The dragon snorted as if in agreement before adding, "Yes. I will return to the skies above us and watch and wait. Stay safe! After all, I am looking forward to a huge snack of acorns when you come out the other end!"

Autumn laughed and went across to him to give him a big kiss on the nose, the flames of her torch reflecting again and again on the hundreds of shiny scales that covered his neck and body.

"You stay safe too! I could not bear it if anything happened to you. Thank you for being my friend!" then as she walked towards Alpha, she grinned back at him, "Never fear, you will be feted with acorns when we are back in the sun again! Farewell!"

It was tough to be continuing without him and she could sense that he stood in the same place for some time watching their retreating backs.

There was just room enough for Blackberry to get through the narrowed tunnel after her. The wolf-cat growled at the sweet sickly smell that greeted them. It made Autumn wretch and hold her hand over her mouth and nose... dead bodies! So Neldon was correct, not all of the soldiers had made it through the tunnel.

A strange sound brought her back into awareness. Something was slithering towards them, something big with glowing bulbous eyes!

CHAPTER THIRTY-ONE

TAN

The plan was a simple one, the Captain would rally his men leaving a small number to follow the librarian's apprentice through the castle to the throne room where the Lord Pretender was currently holding forth.

Meanwhile, the real Lord would request that he be taken to the same room, after all he was the Lord, and should be obeyed, even if he was considered demented.

Tan was still in shock at the thought that Malvic really had and did exist. "Malvic will catch you!" was a game all children played and surely was a figment of everyone's imagination?

But both the Lord and Alton had been sure that the man was supposed to be securely locked away in a prison to the north. It seemed he was a very accomplished magician come wizard and capable of great magic.

"Why was he imprisoned?"

"People began to disappear and many of them were found wandering the wastes of the north with their minds wiped. They could remember nothing of their previous lives and even less of what had happened to them in the time before they were found. It was only when one such person staggered back to their village having escaped capture with a small part of their mind intact and my predecessor was asked to assist with the questioning. Malvic was the name he kept saying, which rang true. Soon after that the hunt began, but it was many years before he was tracked down and put on trial.

He had laughed and laughed at the thought that these lesser people were judging him and boasted that he had been experimenting with the minds of his captives with an aim to harvesting their thoughts."

Alton looked worried as he regaled this story, "I have searched and searched throughout the libraries of the land to find what it was he wanted to achieve by doing this, but there were only guesses that he wished to gain as much knowledge as possible. What was written however, was that the people who had lost their minds were all scholars or people who wielded magic themselves."

He tapped his fingers on his staff which was resting beside him, "Had he been a good man he might have shared his knowledge, but he was not, so as to speak, he dug his own grave. The Lords and judges unanimously agreed that he should be locked away forever."

Lord Nivers interrupted, "Someone must have found a way to break him out – there is no way he could have escaped without help, the prison was secured with magic."

"I agree," Alton had murmured, "but who would do such a thing?"

Lost in thought Tan found he was currently staring at the tangled branches of an old wisteria plant that reached up high to the windows of the Lord's room. The captain had already managed to climb down, swearing comprehensively the whole time.

"Now you, boy!" Alton told him.

* * *

The men had showed no surprise that they were to follow the lead of a youngster, they were well trained and whenever Tan indicated that they should melt into the shadows, to a man, they did just that.

When he reached the kitchens, he went inside alone and quietly asked the cook if she could give him some space, just for a minute or two, because it was better if she was unaware of what was to happen. She bustled out of the kitchen, calling to the two maids who were peeling vegetables at the sink in the nearby room.

The men filed passed, almost silently apart from the odd clink of their swords against their chain-mailed legs.

At the top of the steps Tan guessed he must accept another beating, although it went against the grain to do so, but he was lucky, there was no-one about and it wasn't long before they were standing just around the corner of the throne room. Footsteps and whistling sounded on the stairs coming along the corridor behind them and the man nearest to Tan whipped out his knife.

The first thing that came into sight was a shiny newly

booted foot. That man was despatched very professionally, and Tan was glad it wasn't him that had had to do the deed. Killing someone was not really something he wanted to do.

They waited impatiently for the signal, trying hard not to move any part of their bodies until a loud whistle erupted down the corridor and as a man, they set off in pairs at a pace, with the apprentice trailing close behind them.

The shock on Dintern's face when the soldiers burst into the room was worth seeing and the anger that crossed it when he felt the dagger that Lord Nivers was holding to his neck was even better.

"Tell your men to surrender!" the Lord told the man he had a tight hold on. Alton was beside him, holding his staff aloft ready to repel anyone who was foolish enough to charge at them Dintern said, "You know not what you do! I am protected!"

"Not by me, you're not!" was the gruff response as the fight went out of the pretender.

Tan was still by the doorway when a perfume he recognised came closer to him. The woman was with one of the guards who had so enjoyed giving him a beating. The lad's arm lifted and with a tingling staff he brought it soundly down onto the soldier's head. Crash! The man was out for the count. The woman followed suit without him even touching her. Alton nodded his approval from the other side of the room. The boy did good!

CHAPTER THIRTY-TWO

AUTUMN

The eyes stared into Autumn's as the monster slithered closer and closer and she froze. The wolf-cat on the other hand, did not. She leapt high into the air and slashed at the beast with her claws sinking her jaws into its neck so that with a shrill scream it sank to the ground.

"Thank you, Alpha! What would we have done without you?!"

A purr was the response.

Autumn and the two Fair Folk examined the corpse of the snake, because snake it seemed to be and a huge one at that. Slime oozed from its body making the ground slippery and the smell – well that was totally gross, making them all gag and back away.

"Not nice!!" Lindy announced, "Let's move on, but keep the torches high so we can see what might be confronting us."

They strode off, Blackberry keeping close to his mistress with Alpha on the other side again.

They hadn't gone very far when there was a scream from behind and on turning Autumn was shocked to see that Lindy was suspended high in the air, a very hairy leg wound around her trapping her.

"Oh no!" the red-haired girl muttered, "but where is the body of the beast?"

Ronan stood stock still, his sword held out before him with a dagger in the other hand, surveying what was before them. Even the wolf-cat seemed unsure of what to do.

Autumn put her hand on her longbow and to her surprise it began to glow silver.

"What does that mean?" she asked herself as she pulled it from her shoulders and knocked one of the silver arrows. "I have no idea where to aim."

The bow trembled and she just decided to go with instinct and let the bow do its stuff. Bracing herself she pulled back hard.

"I can't breathe!" Lindy yelled as the leg holding her was tightened and her face began to redden, her breath coming out of her in short pants.

With a twang the arrow flew forward and twisted in the air above them, a bright light shining from it. It raced on and then there was a rather horrible shriek as it reached its target. Lindy crashed to the ground as she was released, and holding her torch aloft, Autumn ran towards where the arrow had met its mark.

"Urggh!" she said as she looked at the now deceased huge spider and although it was something she would rather not have done, she plucked the arrow from its body and wiped it clean on the hairy being in front of her before pushing it back into the quiver. The arrow and longbow dulled back to their usual state.

"That… that was something else," Ronan mumbled as he leant over Lindy, checking she was breathing.

"It was, wasn't it? My grandmother had said that the magic in it makes it perform differently for each owner. Gosh, how right she was!!!"

He waved to Autumn and showed her a gash on Lindy's arm – it was already oozing something smelly.

They stared at one another, both trying not to panic and then crossed to the other side of the passageway to whisper.

"The wound is infected! We need to get out of here and find someone who can help her! And quickly in view of the speed which it has begun to fester!!"

"We'll need to look at the map for the nearest village once we get into the open, but there's no time to do that now. Are you able to gather up a bit of the poison from the beast so if we find a healer they will have more of an idea what it is?" Autumn asked.

The Fair Folk lad was doing just that when a sound distracted them, it was Lindy staggering to her feet.

Ronan rushed back to her side, "You are wounded!" he told her gently, "You need to lay down for a while."

"I'm not resting here, who knows what will come after us next!"

"Well, you cannot walk because that will make the blood flow around your body quicker and the poison that is in you too."

Blackberry's heels clicked as he walked carefully across

to the Fair Folk girl and then he bent his head and gave her a nudge.

"He's telling you something," his mistress told her friend, "You need to ride him. You can just bend down over his neck to get through the low bits."

"But… but I've never ridden a pony before, I'll fall off!"

The pony nickered gently. "He won't let you, just trust him," their leader told her.

It was a struggle to get the girl onto Blackberry's back and into a position where she would not slide off. It was obvious that she was slipping in and out of consciousness and Autumn's gut wrenched with the worry of it.

Onwards they went, the clip clop of the pony's hooves echoing down the tunnel. It seemed so loud.

"Shall we put something on Blackberry's shoes to stop the sound alerting more beasts?" Autumn suggested, and they stopped again to do just that, finding some twine and tearing up a shirt to tie the material onto his feet.

They set off again. It was getting noticeably colder, and their breath was coming out of their mouths looking like steam. Autumn slowed to check on Lindy, making sure she had her cloak wrapped tightly around her body.

"It's OK," the girl murmured, struggling to keep her eyes open, "Blackberry's body is keeping me nice and warm," and she gave him a pat, "Thank you Blackberry for looking after me!"

Autumn tightened her own cloak, shrugging her shoulders up and down to try and release the tension in them as she stared on ahead. Her hand was tightly gripping the longbow in the hope that it might give her any warning of foes heading their way. Alpha left them to scout on ahead and was soon out of sight.

The torches flickered showing up the crevices in the stones each side of them, many had tumbled down from high up in the walls and would be a great hiding place for any beast that was hunting them.

An extremely unpleasant odour wafted towards them – a bit like old rotten meat with dirty socks mixed up in it.

"There must be more remains ahead of us," the leader thought to herself. "How much longer do we have to do this?"

The sound of something scampering towards them had Autumn bring the company to a quick halt, and out of the gloom were two golden eyes heading their way.

"It's Alpha!" she told the others.

But rather worryingly, the wolf-cat seemed a little out of sorts, the fur along her back was up, much like that of a dog when it was aware of something they didn't like.

"Is it safe ahead?" Autumn asked her, running her hand down the animal's back. It was slick with something wet and when Autumn looked at the tips of her fingers they were green.

"Have you just met with one of our enemies, my friend?"

The wolf-cat purred momentarily and then suddenly her hackles came up! At the same time the long-bow gleamed silver and the sounds of scuttling headed towards them.

"Be on guard! There sounds like there is a host of some sort coming our way!"

Lindy slid to the ground and pulled out her sword, leaving her longbow where it was but her arm was shaking and then she collapsed into a heap.

"Let's put her behind that boulder over there! She will be eaten alive if she tries to fight!"

They dragged the sick girl over to the side pulling her cloak around her to keep her hidden.

Autumn returned to the centre of the tunnel, standing tall as she notched an arrow in her own longbow hearing the rasp of Ronan's sword as it came out of its scabbard.

The sounds were getting closer and closer.

What on earth was coming towards them? Alpha growled deep in her throat standing unmoving beside Autumn as Ronan readied himself, his legs apart but balancing on his toes in preparation for what was to come.

Autumn loosed an arrow – the aim was perfect, but it just bounced off of its intended victim.

Ronan muttered quietly, "I don't think that longbow of yours is going to make a difference here! You're going to need your sword!"

Hundreds of huge yellow beetles were heading towards them, their antenna waving excitedly when they spotted the prey ahead of them. Their carapaces gleamed in the light from the torches. How on earth were they going to deal with these when there were only two of them and a wolf-cat to fight them off?!

CHAPTER THIRTY-THREE

TAN

Fortunately, they kept to the footpath near the edge of the forest which meant they were out of sight of the hordes of soldiers who had appeared unexpectedly marching in tight formation.

"Why so many?" Tan asked his Master.

"It does seem overkill, doesn't it?" Alton mused thoughtfully. "They all appear to be heading towards Wick, but the question is, have they already visited Hertle?"

The regularity of their footsteps gave Tan the opportunity to think. He found he missed the company of the wolf-cat.

Then his mind turned to Autumn – he just hoped she'd found safety somewhere.

Finally, to his mum and sister in Wick, and Otto too. He was desperate to get back there and see what was happening in the village.

The small township of Hertle came into view and their arrival was met with smiles and a big welcome, which was so different from the greeting they'd received at Lord Nivers' estate.

Before taking leave of their previous host, Alton and his apprentice had visited the huge library in the castle. Yet again, his Master seemed to know exactly where every book he needed might be found and Tan spent the day going backwards and forwards bringing dusty old tomes to the table where his Master sat chomping on the stem of his old pipe flicking carefully from page to page before ordering his apprentice to return the book to where it had been found. It was a long business but at last as night fell Alton seemed satisfied with his findings.

The guards who'd greeted them advised that the Lord of Hertle's soldiers had easily repelled the incoming force who'd been sent on their way with their tails between their legs.

"So where are we off to now Master?"

"Into danger my boy… into the heart of the enemy."

"Not… not to Wick?"

"Not yet, but never fear, that will come for sure. No, we must try and stem the evil that is before us first, or Wick will never be safe, mark my words."

Tan had to bite his tongue to stop himself protesting because his main worry was his home, but he knew that as an apprentice to Alton he had to follow orders, no matter what he felt about them.

"Now lad, when we stop at our next camp, we must begin our preparations to face the strong magic that will confront us in Malvic's lair where he will no doubt feel safe and which is most possibly the last place he will expect an attack. We must assume that there is the possibility that he has somehow escaped from his prison, but nevertheless he should be unable to breach the magical security wards around the perimeter."

"Yes Master," Tan made sure his voice didn't quaver at the thought.

They followed their usual rituals for camping and soon a fire was blazing, some pieces of meat giving out a fabulous aroma as they roasted. It was drizzling so Tan had expertly erected some makeshift covers over the bracken cushioned beds. He sighed as he did this remembering the comfy bed of the previous night that he'd been allocated.

"Now, my young apprentice, damp or not, prepare yourself and keep your mind open – we will spar!"

Tan found that he could hold his own quite well against his Master which made him smile but then they began some new and rather strange moves using the magic within their staffs. It took a lot of concentration and when Alton finally told him to rest, Tan found his head was spinning and he had to sit down to settle himself.

"We will do that again tomorrow morning and evening because it is essential that you can master that magic before we face our enemy," Alton advised him.

"Oh joy!" was all that Tan could think, he was dreading it.

They set off the next morning, his Master setting a steady but fast pace, with his apprentice jogging alongside. At least he wasn't as puffed as he had been when they had first left Wick.

"Lord Nivers is sending an elite but small bunch of soldiers with Captain Smithers to assist us, as is the Lord of Hertle but we must not rely on them because none of them is capable of using magic and magic is going to be the key to the battle before us."

Tan looked up at the man questionably.

"I know, this seems rather a steep ask of you my boy, but I am sure you are ready for this. You have learned so much in the very short time you have been with me and I must say I never expected that of you."

A brief smile crossed Tan's face at the compliment.

"You are a good teacher Master!"

"Well, we will see on the morrow," was the answer.

CHAPTER THIRTY-FOUR

AUTUMN

Autumn let loose another arrow, but it was to no avail, the shiny covering across the beetles just repelled it.

"It seems you are right!" she called out, pulling her sword out of its sheath to wave it high in the air above her.

"Get ready!"

Alpha barrelled into the first beetle to arrive, its rather revolting looking maw open ready to snatch a bite at its prey. The beetle rolled onto its back, its legs flailing in the air and Ronan leapt forward and sliced downwards with his sword. The sword slid off of the underside of the beetle and he raised his weapon again. The sickening sound of the metal going through the insect's neck was disgusting.

"Cut off their heads!" he shouted, "That's the way to do it!"

Thus began an exhausting exercise of removing the heads from their enemy one by one. Blackberry helped by turning his backside towards the beetles racing towards them and double barrelling them with his hind feet shooting them towards Autumn giving her the means to dispatch them with a flick of her sword.

On the other side, the wolf-cat leapt at them one at a time swiping them sideways so that they would land at Ronan's feet.

The huge insects didn't seem to have enough intelligence to realise what was happening to them despite the huge pile of bodies piling up either side of the tunnel.

It was just too daunting to see how many were coming at them, so Autumn tried to shut out the view down the tunnel and concentrate on the gory massacre. Every now and then a beetle would manage to evade them due to the sheer numbers of them arriving and that would upset the rhythm of the slaughter.

With arms that felt as if they were going to fall off at any moment Autumn called across to the Fair Folk lad, puffing loudly, "Surely, we must be nearly at an end!"

"You would have thought so, wouldn't you!"

Gradually though, they seemed to be winning.

At long last the pair were able to collapse on the ground next to one another. The red-haired girl's arms were shaking with the effort they had been put to.

"I don't think I could manage to behead another one," she panted.

"Me neither!"

Alpha lay down next to them, her coat slick with the slime that the beetles had emitted. Blackberry looked none the better – his legs were green with gunge.

"We couldn't have done that without you both," Autumn told them, "Thank you!"

* * *

It was a great relief to be able to continue their journey but Lindy was comatose on Blackberry's back, which was very worrying. It felt as if they had been travelling in the darkness for an age, just putting one foot in front of the other while keeping watch for any more marauders, until...

"Look!" Autumn shouted exultantly, "There's light – we must be nearing the end of the tunnel!"

The small pinprick of light was getting bigger as they neared it, the air beginning to freshen too, which was something to lift their spirits.

"Thank goodness, but we urgently need to find some help for Lindy," Ronan told her, "She looks close to death!"

To emerge into sunlight was a fabulous feeling and then with a huge gust of wind, Shining Leaves landed next to them.

"Leaf, we are so pleased to see you! But Lindy urgently needs to see a healer. Do you know where the nearest village might be?"

"I will go, let me carry her."

"How?!"

The dragon snatched up the sick girl gently in his front paws and was soon seen getting smaller and smaller until he was just a speck against the clouds.

"At least Lindy won't be aware of where she is," was all Ronan could say worriedly. "I hope they can save her! Let's get away from this horrible place and find somewhere to set up camp. It would be good to wash some of this disgusting gunge off – it stinks!"

* * *

The morning brought no sign of the dragon, but the pair were feeling much better having had their first good night's sleep since they'd left the forest village. Alpha had disappeared off to hunt for food and Blackberry was now his usual gleaming self, which hadn't been a speedy task at all for Autumn.

"Which direction should we set off in?" Ronan asked Autumn, who looked worriedly into the distance where Leaf had disappeared to.

"Well… I guess over that way," and she waved her arm in the general direction that the dragon had disappeared to.

A couple of hours later, not totally sure if they were heading in the right direction, a man appeared from the nearby woods.

"Good morning!" he called cheerfully, "Are you by chance Autumn and Ronan?"

"We are that," was the quick answer, "and you are?"

"I am Fair Folk and the dragon told me to come this way to look for you."

"How… how is Lindy? Is she still alive?" Ronan's voice quavered.

The man smiled back at him, "Follow me and you will soon see! And good day to you too, Blackberry, I have heard much of you, but where is the wolf-cat?"

"She is no doubt hunting, but will be aware of where we are, I'm sure," Autumn replied confidently. The man knew their names and he looked like one of the Fair Folk so they would have to trust him.

When they were deep in the forest a familiar sight greeted them – there was Shining Leaves on his back enjoying the attention he was receiving from young children who were patting his speckled belly and tossing him acorns.

CHAPTER THIRTY-FIVE

OTTO

He stood quietly in the doorway of the library, sunlight brightening the room as it shone through the domed windows.

Yulia was totally unaware of his presence as she studied the book in front of her.

He coughed and startled she looked up.

"Oh Otto! You gave me a fright!"

"It must be interesting, the book you're reading."

"It is… it is one that your librarian suggested I might enjoy and, as usual, he is correct," then she noticed his posture, which was quite stiff, as if he was a little embarrassed.

"Were you looking for me?"

He hesitated before replying, "Yes, I believe I was. I hope I can trust you?"

Smiling back at him she answered, "Yes… I promised that whatever you say will be safe with me."

Otto walked as quietly as he was able down the stone corridor towards the suite of rooms which his parents used. There were no guards in sight. He stopped at the doorway and with a quick glance around him, bent and put his eye to the keyhole.

"Bother!" he muttered, as Yulia had suspected, there was a soldier standing the other side.

He had searched the dungeons prior to going to find his uncle's ward and there had been no sign of the Lord and Lady down there, which in some ways had been worrying because he wondered if they had been put to death. Yulia had reassured him about that having said that she had heard no mention of that happening and she guessed that they were under guard in their suite.

The problem now was that he had no way of speaking to his father to get an idea of what should happen next. He was on his own... although it rather seemed that Yulia might be on his side.

CHAPTER THIRTY-SIX

TAN

They stepped through the stone archway and Tan was shocked at the desolate view before him. Grey rocks littered the ground but there was no sign of any greenery, only greyness. Nothing lived here… nothing at all.

Turning his head to look back through the huge slabs of stone which made up the arched entrance to the area, he could see the soldiers standing ready to repel anything which came towards them.

"Why is there no grass growing this side?" he asked his Master.

"Magic… magic has killed everything that ever lived here. If you look you will see the bones of beasts that are long dead."

"But why?"

"When Malvic was imprisoned, there was a huge fight, wizard against wizard and everything their magic touched withered and died."

The apprentice stared about him, "But where is the prison, Master?"

"In that crater that is straight in front of you, my boy."

They moved carefully forward avoiding the boulders that were in their way until they came to the great hole in the ground. The greyness had disappeared replaced by blackness, much like you would find in a charcoal burner. The air was chill and the sun, which had shone brightly before they had come into this horrible place was no longer in sight.

"See, down there?" Alton pointed his staff and bang in the centre of the crater was a dark shadowy building made out of hewn stone. "That is where we are to meet the enemy. Now, have you readied yourself as I instructed?"

"Yes… yes, Sir!" He gripped his staff tightly in his hand until he felt it tingle in anticipation of what was to come. It seemed his staff was more aware than he was.

It was a bit of a scramble clambering down to the prison, rocks falling away under their feet and rolling with a crash as they landed at the very bottom. Tan kept a sharp eye on where he put his feet as he had no desire to tumble down there himself.

He knew from the lessons that the librarian had given that the actual boundary at the top of the crater had a magical ward surrounding it so that if Malvic somehow managed to escape from where he was entombed, he could go no further.

In the gloom something seemed to move at the edge of Tan's vision.

"Over there! Was it a cloak?" he called to Alton.

"I'm not sure but I saw it too. Keep a sharp eye on it because whoever it is will not be a friend of ours!"

They continued downwards into the stillness below.

The apprentice keeping fairly close to his Master – he was not comfortable here and his instinct was to run and run until he reached the safety of the soldiers.

The prison block itself was made out of huge slabs of blackened stone and the pair circled it tentatively, Alton holding his staff aloft.

"Where is the doorway, Master?" Tan whispered.

The reply was equally quiet, "There is a seam here somewhere which can, if the right words are used, open up to let us in and I'm afraid that is where we must go. Ah, here we are, but… oh dear, as expected someone has got here before us! Look!" In front of them was a yawning gap showing a dark passageway ahead of them.

Suddenly, there was a flash of light behind them and a piece of the stone next to them sheered off, shattering on the ground.

"Keep your head down and step into the passageway!"

Alton then uttered some mysterious words before saying, "That should hold it open!"

Coldness seemed to emanate around them.

"Don't go any further because my guess is it will be booby trapped and the last thing we want is to be caught in here. Let us see who or what it is that is attacking us."

They both hunkered down and peered carefully around the edge of what had been the doorway.

"Over there, Master! Can you see someone just behind that huge boulder?"

"I can indeed. Gather up some of these small rocks and if we lob them towards whoever it is, and I guess it might well be Malvic himself, we may distract them and then we must run... and run very fast! Each of us must go either side of him."

Tan did as he was instructed, piling rocks at their feet and then clasping one firmly in his hand, waiting for his Master's command.

"After three! One, two, three!"

Each of them lobbed a rock in the air and then used their staffs to spin the missiles towards their target and then they both ran!

Tan sped forward, bending low and ducked down behind a boulder and just in time it seemed, when a sheet of flame shot across towards him. He flung himself down on the ground waiting for the signal from the librarian, which would be a few stars sprinkled into the sky, like a firework.

There it was! And the battle commenced.

Both Tan and Alton were shouting magical words as they pointed their staffs directly at their opponent, light pulsing forward and melding into a circle around their prey. Malvic might be a strong magician but the band of light grew and grew into a huge manacle that began to move the wizard back towards his prison.

It took a lot of concentration for Tan to keep his staff steady, but they appeared to be winning!

Just when it seemed that Malvic was about to be totally trapped within their magic a spark of light arrowed into the magical ring... and it died!

Why?

A woman with long golden hair stepped into view, beams of light coming strongly out of the wand that she had out before her.

"Imelda!" Alton shouted in surprise, "What are you doing here?"

"It is time for my long lost love to be free again and for us to rule the land side by side!"

CHAPTER THIRTY-SEVEN

AUTUMN

The decision to leave her Fair Folk friends and head onwards had been a hard one, but Autumn was sure she was doing the right thing. After all, her plan always had been to catch up with Tan and Alton and then the three of them could come up with a plan to rescue the villagers of Wick. In reality it sounded a bit ambitious but she was very determined.

Lindy was still weak but the healer in the village certainly knew her stuff and as soon as she had examined the glob of gunge that they'd collected she set down to work. She had every confidence in Lindy making a full recovery.

"You must stay with her, Ronan," Autumn told him. "She will need you!"

"But... you should not go on alone!"

"I have company remember, I have the brave Alpha, Blackberry and Shining Leaves who will guide me."

The sound of jaws snapping in the air made them both

laugh as the dragon caught another flying acorn, it seemed he was getting quite adept at it.

"I must gather some acorns for him as I had promised," Autumn said quietly.

"Are you sure you will be alright?" Ronan asked.

"That's a silly question! Who knows?! But what I do know is that my companions will do their best to protect me, won't you Leaf?"

A burst of flame seemed to be the answer as the wolf-cat wound herself around the girl's legs purring loudly. Blackberry neighed.

"There you are! That's your answer, Ronan!"

The dragon suddenly jumped up, lifting his snout high in the air.

"We must away! I sense something is amiss with the magic of the world!"

They left immediately, Autumn keeping a close eye on Shining Leaves who was high in the sky – he knew where they were needed.

As she had readied herself to mount Blackberry, a child had tapped her on the leg and smiling shyly handed Autumn a heavy bag. On looking inside she was over the moon to see it was full of fresh acorns.

"We know you haven't had time to collect any, so we did it for you!" the girl lisped at her. "Just don't tell the dragon that it was us!" and she giggled quietly.

"Oh, thank you so much! That is amazing! A wondrous gift to be sure."

She tucked the bag away carefully in one of the saddle bags and swung herself up into the saddle, her bow across her shoulders.

The wolf-cat skulked away into the undergrowth, but Autumn knew she remained close by.

They travelled at a good pace stopping only to give the pony a short rest and for Autumn to fill up her water bottle from the same stream that Blackberry drank from.

Shining Leaves stayed high above them keeping a sharp eye on their surroundings, but where they were heading, she had no idea because it seemed to her that they were by-passing Hertle. Every now and then he would make a wide circle which Autumn assumed was so that Blackberry could keep up with him.

They kept just inside the treeline to avoid the occasional marching soldiers who were heading in the opposite direction.

Finally, Shining Leaves turned slightly to the north, was he looking for somewhere to camp perhaps? The girl was rather hoping for a rest.

It seemed that was not going to be the case as the dragon continued onwards, too far away to ask.

At long last he swept down, some way in front of them and it was good to find him waiting patiently for them.

"Are we camping here?" Autumn asked him.

"No, but I must now continue on foot as we are nearing our destination. Is your bow ready should it be needed?"

"Yes, it is." Fortunately, the Fair Folk had refilled her quiver after the horrible experience in the tunnel.

"Let us go, but keep your eyes peeled," which was a strange thing for a dragon to say and she wondered where he had heard it before.

Autumn was now marching just behind the dragon,

making sure she didn't tread on his long tail which would flick up every now and then.

"There are people ahead," she called to him quietly.

Surely the dragon smirked – could a dragon do that? "I know! They are soldiers and their livery is that of Lord Nivers and of Hertle."

It wasn't the time to question how on earth he knew that, but he seemed to be full of information today.

A soldier moved away from his men and raised his hand to his head.

"Well met young lady. I am Captain Smithers and the librarian told us to expect you." He didn't seem fazed by the sight of the dragon or even flinch when Alpha crept out of the bushes and settled down beside Autumn.

It didn't seem the time to question how they knew she was coming but it brought a smile to the girl's face, because at long last it looked like she had finally caught up with Tan.

"So, why are you waiting here?"

"Alton instructed us to guard that entrance over there!"

Shining Leaves bent his long neck and looked into her eyes.

"We too, have to go through that archway but I can sense loose magic and much danger. I believe it is where I felt the ripple in the magic that I told you about."

Autumn pulled the long bow from her shoulders and knocked an arrow. The bow shivered and turned silver in her hand making the captain's eyes widen at the sight of it.

"Let us go then! If Tan needs help, we should be there to give it to him!"

Shining Leaves led the way through the archway

and Autumn was shocked when she saw how the terrain altered from that of lush greenness to grey stone. Flashes of red light bounced up in the air in front of them.

Magic!

CHAPTER THIRTY-EIGHT

TAN

It was a herculian effort to try to keep hold of his staff and the magic he could feel inside it was surprisingly feeble. What was happening? He and his Master were being herded very slowly back towards the prison! This strange woman was strong with magic.

Imelda cackled loudly. "It will be your turn to be trapped inside that place and my love will be free to roam by my side!" As she spoke what looked like a wizard stepped from behind a nearby boulder and sparks flew from the end of his fingers towards Alton. They were blocked, but only just.

"There you are!" Alton shouted lifting his staff and waving it towards the wizard. "So… it is you that has been attempting to take over the castles?"

"What do you mean, attempting! I have been succeeding!" was the angry retort.

"I would not put it that way myself! Hertle is free and Lord Nivers is no longer under the spell of that idiot, Dintern!" growled Tan's Master.

"There is still Wick!"

"That there is, but what do you expect to happen there?"

The woman pushed her blond hair out of her eyes, her wand still held steadily in front of her.

"My love, can you see that he is trying to distract you!" she exclaimed, "Not that there will be anyone coming to help them!"

She waved the wand so that magic shoved them a step further back, more sparks tumbling out of the tips of Malvic's fingers.

Tan stumbled when he felt the wave of magic hit him and he fell to the ground.

"Get up, boy! Get up now or die!" his Master ordered.

He very slowly dragged himself to his feet, feeling frightened because he could see that Alton was struggling to resist the magic that was coming from Malvic's fingers.

Another step forward, and another and another and then he had to put his hand out to stop himself being moved into the open door of the prison.

"No! I am not going to let myself be entombed in there! It would be forever! Push back!" he told himself and with that he made an effort to mentally resist the magic that was flowing into him from the woman's wand. His staff shuddered in his hand and a flood of magic burst from it giving him a brief respite from the attack.

Alton too, was fighting back and kept muttering what must be magical words to try and break through his opponent's constant flow of magic.

161

Suddenly, out of nowhere a silver arrow shot through the sky piercing Imelda's shoulder making her scream with pain. It gave Tan time to dodge away from the gaping doorway. Another arrow sliced through Imelda's thigh and then a wolf-cat leapt upon her and ripped out her throat, blood spurting high and far.

"No, not my Imelda! You will pay for this!" yelled Malvic readying his other hand to add to the flow of evil magic that was pulsing from his fingertips. A few stars spluttered in the air but possibly the emotion of losing his love had unsettled him, but before he could do any more there was a loud roar and flames engulfed him as a dragon appeared on the top of the slabs of rock on the prison's roof.

The dragon continued to burst fire at the wizard and then with a bang, Malvic disappeared from sight.

Tan started to drag himself to his feet when a soft voice said in his ear, "Here, let me help you!" and he spun around as a pair of arms circled him giving him an enormous hug.

"Autumn…? How… how on earth did you get here? And what is Alpha doing with you?"

A pony neighed loudly a little way off and Tan realised that Blackberry was there too.

He almost collapsed from shock, but Autumn's arms were strong as she made sure he remained upright.

"We have much to tell you, and you have a story to relate as well," she told him quietly, "but I am so pleased to find you alive. Shining Leaves was sure we needed to come here urgently, and it seems he was right!"

"Shining Leaves?"

"The acorn loving dragon!" she giggled.

Leaf turned his head and stared at her, "Don't forget you owe me!" he growled.

* * *

It was sometime later that they left the scene of destruction, Alton having sealed the prison, "Just in case!" he said. They left the remains of the wizard's accomplice where they had fallen, none of them wanting to go near them, but the one other task the librarian performed was to collect Imelda's wand and ask Shining Leaves to destroy it completely.

"Is that the end of Malvic?" the apprentice questioned tentatively.

"That I do not know, although my gut feeling is that he has somehow escaped. I would very much like to be wrong on that score but it could be that Imelda's magic somehow rent a hole in the wards allowing him to get away."

"How... how could he manage to organise the assault on the various castles if he was imprisoned here?"

"Another question that I do not know the answer too... although, I seem to recollect that in one of the tomes I have studied there is a way of using telepathy or even dream walking to communicate. That is something I will have to investigate further once we have dealt with the problems of Wick. Come now... let us leave this desolate place."

Captain Smithers was delighted to see them all return through the gateway safely, obviously longing to know what had occurred, but Alton waved him away.

"We need to set up camp, but not so close to this entranceway please. My apprentice is very tired, so not too far away either," he winked at Tan.

The soldiers were well trained and soon the campfire was blazing, with a little help from Shining Leaves who then left to hunt for food. Alpha too, was nowhere to be seen.

Tan was longing to just sit and just do nothing, but his Master had other ideas.

"Before you rest you must perform your exercises or your muscles will sieze up, they have been through much today."

His apprentice groaned, but he joined Alton in the stretching sequences, totally blown away when Autumn joined them by performing similar stances.

The moon was high in the sky once they were finally able to go to rest their weary heads, having spent some considerable time exchanging tales of their exploits.

CHAPTER THIRTY-NINE

OTTO

There was a feeling deep in his boots that he needed to act... now. He still hadn't formulated a plan but with his father being inaccessible and therefore unable to guide him, it was time to step up into the role of son of the Lord. It was his castle and his people.

He marched down towards the dining area and tried not to grimace when he saw his uncle seated at the table clicking his fingers at the nearby servants to order food to be served. At his side was his advisor, a man dressed totally in black with greasy black hair. He looked totally untrustworthy as far as Otto was concerned.

"Nephew! We couldn't wait any longer for you... sit and my manservant, Groller will serve you your first course."

Otto settled himself on a seat opposite the pair, which happened to be next to Yulia. She smiled faintly at him as she broke a piece of bread and rolled it in her fingers.

"Oh!" she cried as she rather clumsily knocked over her goblet of wine, quickly producing a napkin to start dabbing at the wetness. As she did so she turned her head towards Otto whispering, "Do not drink the wine! Pretend!" and then continued mopping up the wine.

The soup, when it arrived was still warm and tasty, which Otto would have expected as it was made by the cook who had been in service to his father for years.

Groller poured him some wine and waited for him to taste it, as was normal.

His uncle's ward kept her gaze firmly on her own soup but under the table her foot nudged his as he raised the goblet to his lips. He made sure the liquid did not touch his mouth as he put the wine back on the table, nodding his approval at the manservant who bent over and filled it to the brim.

The conversation during dinner was desultory and rather boring, although Otto rather enjoyed asking his uncle how his father and mother were faring.

The man winced at the question before replying smoothly that they were in good health and he need not concern himself about them.

It was tricky trying to look as if he was drinking the wine, but he managed to pour a little of it discreetly into his soup bowl and then leave a piece of bread over the remains. Likewise with the main course which was rather helpfully stewed beef. Groller refilled his goblet when his uncle proposed a toast to Yulia, saying that she looked rather beautiful tonight.

The girl blushed and smiled accepting the compliment, giving Otto another nudge with her foot to remind him not to sip any of the wine.

Finally, they were given permission to leave the room and Otto asked Yulia if she would like a little stroll in the castle gardens to help her meal go down. His uncle looked on approvingly when she accepted with alacrity and ordered one of the servants to fetch her a cloak.

It was some while before they could speak openly, having to wait until they were a distance away from the castle.

"Why are you helping me?"

She looked down at her feet as if considering her response, "There are two parts but I will only give you the answer to one at the moment."

He drew in a breath… inhaling the scent of orange blossom.

"I do not agree with what is happening here at the castle… he is not the right person to be Lord… he… he does not have the qualities or ethics of a true leader, unlike your father and yourself."

"Me! You believe that I am a true leader."

She smiled gently at him, "Of course! You have just needed time to grow into the role."

Otto felt shocked, how could she know what he was when his uncle just considered him to be a weak fool. The only sound that could be heard was that of their footsteps on the small pathway they were following, until eventually he drew breath and asked.

"And the second part of your answer?"

"Ah… I will keep that to myself for now because you are not yet ready to hear it!"

Time to change the subject then as he wondered what on earth she might have been thinking.

"What was wrong with the wine?" he asked.

"I believe it had a sleeping draught in it. Have you not noticed that you are sleeping more soundly than usual of late? I know I have."

He gave it some thought before answering, "You are quite right… how could I not have realised that. Quite often one of the maids has to wake me. How did you know?"

"I thought I saw Groller tipping something into one of the decanters earlier this evening. He wasn't aware of my being in one of the armchairs beside the fire."

"Yulia! Thank you… but why is he doing that?"

"If everyone is sleeping soundly in their beds, they cannot be out causing trouble I guess."

Otto sighed, "I think it is time that I need to shake the tree a little but although I have been wracking my brains, I cannot decide what to do that will not cause a problem for my people."

She touched his arm gently, "Your heart is in the right place, Otto. Why don't you take it one step at a time? You know your captain of the guards is in one of the dungeons?"

"Yes, I've been down there to check how many people are imprisoned."

They walked a little further before turning back towards the castle, neither of them wanting to be out so long that someone would be sent to check on them.

"Go down there in the middle of the night and see if you can talk to him and it is possible that he may well have an idea of how to aid you."

CHAPTER FORTY

AUTUMN

She snuggled down on the bed of bracken, her cloak pulled up around her neck. The wolf-cat's body was tucked up beside her acting like a hot water bottle by her side. Tan snorted when he saw her sleeping companion.

"How come she is with you now?" he complained.

Alpha purred, obviously enjoying being the centre of attention. She rose to pad across and gave Tan a raspy lick of her tongue, he didn't dare complain about the smell of raw meat on her breath just giving her a friendly pat, but then she returned to her previous position beside Autumn.

Shining Leaves snores reverberated loudly from the other side of the camp, a pile of acorns between his great talons. He was leaving guarding the perimeter to the soldiers.

Autumn smiled, ruffling the wolf-cat's fur. Tomorrow they would start the trek back to Wick and she was longing to see her parents again.

The sun was glowing low in the sky when Autumn edged out from under her cloak, leaving Alpha comatose. She saw that Alton and Tan were about their exercises and she joined them as she did the forms which Allina, the warrior of the Fair Folk had taught her. Some of the soldiers had watched briefly before following their example beginning to spar with one another, Captain Smithers being one of them. Soon the sound of heavy breathing and clashing swords filled the air.

Alpha was oblivious to it all, and of Shining Leaves there was no sign.

Breakfast was eaten in companionable conversation, with Alton filling in Captain Smithers with the bare outline of what had passed the previous day. He kept a lot of the details to himself, after all, he was supposedly just a librarian.

Once she'd groomed Blackberry and checked his tack was in good condition Autumn stowed her bedding away, ensuring that if it rained it would be kept dry.

"Form up!" the captain ordered his men. It was interesting to see that the soldiers from Hertle were happy to accept his commands. All in all there were just twenty of them, but they were a sturdy bunch who looked well-campaigned and ready for anything that came their way.

The mule seemed quite content too and they were soon on their way. Two of the soldiers had been sent to scout ahead, the rest marching in pairs, keeping their eyes peeled for anything unusual they might come across.

Tan walked next to his Master for a short while but then dropped back to be with Autumn who was riding Blackberry, the wolf-cat padding along next to them.

"Alpha must have understood that I was concerned about you," the lad said to his friend, "she disappeared not long after I had told her about you."

The girl smiled back at him as the wolf-cat purred as if in agreement.

"How did you come across Shining Leaves, as you call him?"

She went on to explain that because she had been bored, she had gone searching for the dragon for something to do.

"Where is he by the way?" Tan asked as he stared up into the sky looking for a sight of the beast.

"I guess he is off to see how the land lays ahead and what we might have to face on the journey," she replied. "When I was on my own, he would make sure he was in sight so that I could follow him and he could help if he was needed, but I guess he feels I'm in safe company."

Tan looked serious as he said, "You have been very brave!"

"What else could I do? It was no good crying and hoping someone would rescue me. I was trying to reach you and Alton, but I made some surprisingly good friends on the way."

There was a shout from ahead and the column of soldiers came to a halt, and Alpha left her side and padded off.

"I wonder what's happening?" Autumn said worriedly, "I hope it's not trouble."

She led Blackberry past the men and was astounded when she saw who was waiting at the side of the pathway.

"Ronan... how come you are here?" and then in

a quavery and emotional voice, "And Lindy!" and she dropped from Blackberry's back and ran forward to grab hold of her friend and give her a big hug. "You are well?"

"We couldn't let you have all the fun!" Lindy laughed in her ear.

CHAPTER FORTY-ONE

TAN

He had to squash the green-eyed monster that had risen when he saw how comfortable Autumn was with Ronan. Now was not the time to be jealous.

As they set off again Autumn and Ronan told of the monsters they had had to face in the tunnel, making sure that Alpha and Blackberry's part in the adventure was mentioned. The wolf-cat purred whenever her name came up, waving her tail like a wand in the air. The pony would snort his approval too.

Tan hadn't been told the exact details of the trip through the tunnel when they had been exchanging stories the night before, and he was shocked to hear how near to death they had come. It was no wonder that Autumn and Ronan were quite close, that kind of experience bonded people.

There was a feeling of light-heartedness when they camped that night and Ronan, rather surprisingly, brought a harmonica to his mouth and played a jig with Lindy's musical voice singing the lyrics. Shining Leaves had returned and was watching the events closely. After Lindy had finished her song, claiming she was thirsty and needed ale, one of the soldiers launched into a rather bawdy ballad which had the whole camp roaring with laughter.

The moonlight was shining on them when they finally settled down to sleep, but Tan found it difficult to close his eyes, his head being full of everything that had occurred over the past days and the fear of what was ahead.

The plan was quite a simple one – Tan and Autumn were to enter the castle and alert Otto, assuming of course that he was still free to wander where he wished at will. Once they had more information on how the land lay, they were then to return and report to the librarian.

It sounded too easy, particularly as they had to get past the many soldiers that would be camped near the village.

Alton had tried to sooth their fears, "Remember that most of the soldiers you will come across are in the main mercenaries, men who have been hired. They are likely to be rough sorts, but I am sure you will be able to deal with them if you need to. Remember, you have faced far worse before and this time there will be no magic involved."

But what the librarian didn't realise was that his apprentice's biggest worry was, would he be capable of protecting Autumn?

* * *

It was dusk when the pair began to creep towards the village. The sentries were set a couple of hundred yards apart but most of them stood staring unseeingly away from the village, some with a cigarette hanging from their lips and a few others swigging from a hipflask. It took little skill to weave their way past them.

"The forge first," Autumn whispered, "and let's hope my parents are there because they may be able to tell us what to expect in the castle."

Tan nodded – this course of action had been agreed at their planning meeting.

Sounds coming from the forge were a surprise because in the past Autumn's father had closed up shop when the light faded. As they neared it she could see his strong arms raising a hammer and bringing it down onto the metal he was moulding on his anvil. Red sparks flew here and there around him. Her heart swelled at the sight of him, but then a movement in the shadowy rear of the forge alerted her to the fact that someone was with him.

Tan touched her arm indicating that they should slip around the side of the building. He glanced up in the sky briefly and smiled as he saw the shape of a dragon flying above them.

"Wait!" Autumn whispered, "Leaf says to hide!"

They slipped quietly into the nearby undergrowth and just in time, as the sound of marching boots came towards them and a couple of soldiers came into view, laughing loudly as they dragged a young girl along with them. She looked terrified!

"What do you suggest we do?" Autumn asked her companion, "That's Susannah the groundsman's daughter. We can't leave her!"

"You're right!" Tan had some quick thinking to do and

the only thing he could think of was not anything he had attempted before. "Wait here and stay out of sight! I am going to try something but if it goes wrong, grab her and get her to safety."

He moved silently forward gripping his staff firmly in his hand feeling its tingling response.

He gave no warning but lifted the staff up, keeping it vertical and then in time with the ringing sound coming from the forge, banged it down hard. A flash of light shot out from the magical piece of wood and much to Tan's surprise the soldiers both crashed to the ground, as did the girl.

"Quickly!" he called to Autumn, "We need to move them out of sight."

She didn't hesitate and ran to his side to grab the legs of one of the men. "Where?"

"Into that ditch just down there."

It took a big effort to shift the men because they were not lightweights, but eventually they managed it.

"Are… are they still alive?"

"I think so, but now we need to get Susannah to safety. Will your mother take her in?"

CHAPTER FORTY-TWO
AUTUMN

Much to her surprise her mother was waiting in the open doorway of the cottage. Autumn wanted to run and rush into her arms but now was not the time.

"Bring her inside, as quick as you can!" her mother told her looking a little grim. "We will hide her in your room. Hurry!"

As soon as the door was closed, Tan lifted the comatose girl in his arms and carried her up the stairs, waiting at the top to be told where to go.

"In there!"

She was laid down on the bed and Autumn's mother pressed an ear to her chest.

"She is breathing as if she's asleep. Do… do you know how long she will remain like this?"

"I think it should be a few hours, but I'm not sure as I've never done what I did before," Tan replied.

"Well, I won't ask what it was because after all you are the librarian's apprentice, are you not?" and she smiled and then swept her daughter into her arms.

A big sob came from the girl as she gripped her mother tightly. "How did you know we were here?"

"Fair Folk have a second sense about these things."

"I am so pleased to see you! Are you and dad both alright?"

"Your father made it very clear to the new Lord of the Castle that if anyone so much as laid a finger on me he would not work, and whoever it was would be dealt with."

Autumn smiled at that, it sounded much like what her grandmother had told her would have happened and she wished she could stay in the comforting embrace of her mother but there was no time, they had to move on.

Having gathered as much information as they were able to about where the soldiers were bunked down and who might be in the castle dungeons, it was time to leave.

The woman touched the longbow which hung over her daughter's shoulders. "I can tell this was meant for you to wield and its magic will work for you in a different way than it would have done for me, you must have met your grandmother again."

"That I have," Autumn noticed the sadness that flashed across her mother's face. "Don't worry about me, after all I have Tan and his staff to look after me," she grinned, "but we need to be moving so that we can return to the camp before sunrise.

After another cuddle, they were soon jogging up the road leading to the castle, Shining Leaves having reported that the way was clear so in no time at all they were at the foot of the rowan tree.

"You first!" she told Tan, "Shining Leaves is keeping an eye out for us and will let me know if there is any trouble approaching," and with that she settled herself on one of the lower branches.

The moon shone down on them helping Tan find his footholds as he scrambled up, following the same route that they would have done in their younger years. He gave a short whistle when he reached the top alerting Autumn that it was now her turn. When she reached him she found him struggling to open the window a little wider.

"Here, let me go first, you must have grown a bit since we were last here," she giggled quietly. The window had always been kept open because Otto liked the fresh air that would blow in, no matter whether it was summer or winter.

Handing him her longbow, she shimmied through the gap and then gave the window a good hard shove. It creaked as it moved so she put up a hand to stop Tan from climbing through in case anyone had heard the noise.

The sound of snoring came from the room the other side of the door and when she peeked through the gap, she could see Otto's form under the covers spreadeagled out across the whole bed.

Back by the window she took her longbow from Tan and waited while he clambered in to join her.

"We'll need to wake him!" the girl muttered.

"You'd be the best one to do that, in case he's still annoyed with me."

The Lord's son spluttered awake when Autumn nudged

179

his shoulder and she had to press her hand over his mouth to stop him from crying out.

"It's me! Be quiet! I'll take my hand away in a moment!" she whispered in his ear. "Tan's here with me."

Otto sat up, wiping the sleep from his eyes.

"What are you doing here! You'll be caught and I won't be able to help you!"

"Let's talk and we'll tell you what's been happening as concisely as we can and then you can explain what the situation is within the castle."

CHAPTER FORTY-THREE

TAN

There were faces he didn't know when they finally reached the camp... and just in time before the sun began to colour the sky pink, but Autumn seemed to know them and greeted them with a beaming face.

"You came!"

"Of course, you will need our numbers to help quell the soldiers that are camped just inside the village walls."

It seemed the man that spoke was the leader of the group who had arrived during the night and he had a warrior with him.

"And this is Allina, the Fair Folk's general," Autumn told the apprentice.

Alton took charge of the conflab that followed – rather surprising for a man who was known to be a librarian, Tan thought, but Neldon seemed quite happy to bow to his leadership.

The wolf-cat prowled into the centre of the pow-wow rubbing her body against the Fair Folk's leader's legs. She received a gentle stroke of her back before she moved over to settle down next to Autumn.

Blackberry was also close by, munching quietly on some grass but Tan could see that his ears were flicking to and fro as if he too was listening. Then before they got down to the nitty-gritty the dragon glided into the clearing, landing quietly before almost sashaying across to them.

"All is quiet amongst the soldiers," he told Autumn.

"The fire in the forge was damped down when we went past on our return," she replied.

"Yes, but…there is movement in the village, shadows going from house to house, not troops, they are much too quiet to be them." the dragon added so all could hear. "I could hear them whispering as they too, are preparing for the fight which is to come."

The red-haired girl felt her heart sink to her boots, she didn't want her family to face danger and risk being killed, but then she supposed her parents would feel the same about her.

"We should launch an attack immediately, before the soldiers have time to wake properly. Neldon, Allina and Captain Smithers, I will leave it to you to deal with the enemy troops, because you are best placed to do so. Hopefully, you will come across men who are loyal to Lord Travers senior, and these could help the villagers that the blacksmith is rallying."

Tan interrupted him.

"We forgot to tell you that Otto has already managed

to release the Captain of the Guard from the dungeons who is sending out someone to find Leonard, my brother where he is in hiding with some of the other men. It is hoped they too, will join the fray."

"That is good news," his Master said before continuing, "Tan, you and Autumn will accompany me, but as my days of climbing trees is long gone, I will enter through the servants' doorway and go up through the library. I will meet you in the musician's gallery above the main hall and we will start our fight from there."

He glanced at the wolf-cat but she was looking at the dragon, as if they were communicating in some way.

Blackberry neighed.

"Ah, yes my friend, you too will have a part to play, let me whisper in your ear." Tan was intrigued but it was obviously going to be a surprise.

* * *

The two friends were yet again climbing the rowan tree but this time the window was ajar and wide enough to let even Tan through. Otto was pacing up and down across his bedroom.

"What took you so long!" he said quietly. "I've been waiting and waiting!"

"Let us tell you the plan," Tan told him and once they had gone through what should now be happening, he asked if the messenger had found Leonard.

"Yes, and he will be joining the battle against the enemy troops. Can we go now? I am coming along to the musician's gallery. I need to be part of this."

Tan looked at Autumn… this was a different person to the lad they had left behind. He seemed to have grown up.

The three of them stopped when they reached the doorway to the bedroom and looked at one another. Standing In a circle they held out their hands, much as they remembered doing when they were up to mischief in their younger days.

"May we cause as much mayhem as possible!" which had been their mantra in those times.

Otto added, "Thank you, both of you for being true friends. I will not forget! And, Tan, I am so sorry for treating you the way I did before you left, that was very wrong of me."

"It's in the past now and there are much more important matters to deal with. Let's go!"

* * *

The only sign of life as they traversed the corridors heading towards the musicians' gallery were servants going about their business. The maids bobbed a curtesy when they saw the young Lord coming towards them and the male servants gave a small bow.

"Luckily, my uncle has not dispensed with the services of the usual staff. They were all given the choice and decided to continue as they were but I know they are loyal to my father and have just been biding their time, waiting to see what transpires."

They slunk into the musicians' gallery, Tan nearly tripping over a lone ukulele that had been left there for some reason. He managed to catch it before it made a sound and alerted the people he could hear below.

Alton was waiting for them in the shadowy corner on the balcony watching the comings and goings of staff and the man who was seated proudly in the throne type seat in the centre of the room.

It might be early in the day but he was barking orders to the servants who were rushing about. All Tan could think was that this was not the orderly and quiet way Otto's father had of dealing with things.

The librarian spoke quietly to the Lord's son, who nodded and slipped from the balcony.

Autumn and Tan exchanged looks – it was time.

CHAPTER FORTY-FOUR

AUTUMN

The arrow flew straight and true landing in the so-called Lord's shoulder, exactly where Alton had wanted it to go.

The man screamed and clutched at the silver missile, nearly falling from his chair as he did. The guards that were close by raised their weapons looking around to see who it was they were to protect him from, but by then Autumn had shifted to the other side of the balcony.

The wounded man yelled for reinforcements and soldiers randomly rushed into the hall, none of them had their weapons to hand – these were not trained men.

Alton nodded again at Autumn and another arrow sped away from her and landed in the man's leg.

"Get it out! Get it out!" he shouted as one of the men gripped hold of the arrow embedded in the leg and pulled.

Alton called down, "I wouldn't do that if I were you, laddie. You will cause more harm than good and if the arrowhead comes through you will kill the man!"

Otto's uncle was sobbing from the pain as he lay on the floor.

"Put down your weapons!" the librarian's voice echoed throughout the room. "If you do not then you will have to bear the consequences of your actions! Once you have done just that, move over to the far corner of the room and do not move until I tell you to."

The man in pain told the soldiers that anyone who surrendered would not be paid, but at that point the wolf-cat made an appearance through the main doorway. With a look of sheer fear there was the crash of swords and daggers as about a third of the soldiers dropped their weapons.

"Don't say I didn't warn you!" Alton called out nodding at his apprentice. Sheets of light filled the whole area below them and to a man, the soldiers collapsed.

"Go down and check if any of them are still conscious please?" he asked Autumn and Tan who promptly left the musician's balcony, moving swiftly down the stone steps nearby.

Once Autumn reached the bottom, with a loud purr Alpha leapt across the room to stay by her side, in case she might be needed to despatch anyone who was a threat.

Voices in the hallway announced some new arrivals and Otto burst into the room, followed closely by his father and more surprisingly, Yulia. Both men were armed but stopped dead in their tracks when they saw the false Lord lying on the floor.

Lord Travers marched across the room and stood over his brother menacingly.

"How dare you imprison me in my own castle!" he roared angrily. His brother's body quivered on the ground as he replied, "Please... please can you get these out? I am in agony!"

"In good time, at the moment we have to ensure the castle is secure and the villagers are all safe."

"Please...!"

"Son, please could you summon a healer, and one of our own to guard my brother. He is not to be trusted."

The Lord then turned to Alton who now stood next to him.

"Thank you, Librarian. Do you know how the rest of the village fares?"

"We should have a report soon, my Lord."

No-one noticed the one soldier amongst the comotose men suddenly leap out straight towards Autumn, a lethal looking knife in his hand. She pulled backwards in an attempt to dodge the sharp blade but quick as a flash a large ball of fur leapt up and intercepted the thrust with a growl. A fountain of blood spurted up high in the air as the man fell to the ground.

"Are you alright?" Tan looked worried as he rushed across to the body of the soldier kicking the dagger far across the floor. Autumn joined him and bent down to the wolf-cat who looked up at her with soft eyes.

"Thank you, my friend! You saved me!" but then she realised that the blood was still leaking onto the floor, and it wasn't coming from the soldier – it was the wolf-cat's blood.

"Tan! Help me!" she panicked. "Alpha has been stabbed by the blade instead of me!"

The pair of them heaved the animal onto her back shocked to find a deep slice going into her belly.

With a big sigh, Alpha closed her eyes.

"No!" Autumn screamed.

At the same time an alien sound echoed from the corridor and Lord Travers and his son both raised their weapons ready to repel whatever it was coming their way.

A large maw with huge yellow teeth appeared in the doorway on the end of a long sinewy scaled neck.

Otto dashed forward ready to slash his sword at the beast, but Shining Leaves just pushed him over with his snout.

Alton smothered a laugh as he told the lad that this was a friend.

"So, this is what a castle looks like inside, what a strange place to want to be." the dragon spoke the words so that everyone in the hall could hear him. Total shock was written on every face in the room. A talking dragon!

"It's cold in here," Leaf said as he snorted flames at the logs that were laid in the fireplace.

"I can't feel her heart!" Autumn sobbed. "She must be dead!"

CHAPTER FORTY-FIVE

TAN

He bent low over Alpha, putting his arm around the sobbing Autumn trying to give her comfort. They were both covered in the wolf-cat's blood.

Alton huffed and went to speak in a low voice to the dragon, but they could all hear what he said.

"I have read... Shining Leaves, that dragons have a special magic that can heal if the recipient is another magic user."

Leaf waved his head about closing his eyes as he did, as if examining some memory or thought.

Tan waited with Autumn as they stared hopefully at the dragon.

It seemed like forever before he replied, "Yes, I believe you are correct, Librarian."

"Move away from her," Shining Leaves growled.

Obediently they shuffled backwards, loathe to leave

the body of the big animal on its own. She had been a good friend to them.

Gradually a humming and warmth filled the room… a lot of heat and Tan pulled at his jumper trying to release some of the sweat which was beginning to run down his neck. It got hotter, and hotter and one of the Lord's soldiers crashed to the ground in a faint.

There was yet more heat, but no flames accompanied it, just smoke from Shining Leaves' nostrils. He looked formidable as he concentrated, even the horns on top of his head began to shake with the effort he was having to make.

Alpha's body gave a shudder and then stilled again.

More of that heat filled the room.

Another tremble and then…

Autumn gripped Tan's hand hard, digging her nails in until he winced.

"Oh, sorry," she muttered as she released her hold on him.

They both stared across at the wolf-cat, willing her to come back to them.

A tremble ran from the animal's head to her tail and then… she stretched out as if sleeping.

"You can go to her now," the dragon told them and that was all the pair needed to rush across the room and examine her.

"I can feel her heart beating and she's breathing! And… the bleeding has stopped!"

Tan ran his hand over the soft belly. Where was the cut?

"It's gone!" he said, looking back at the dragon. "You have healed her!!"

But Shining Leaves' eyelids closed and his head crashed to the ground, making everyone jump before he began to snore – very loudly. The sound echoing around them.

Lord Travers and Otto stood rooted to the spot, totally shocked and unable to utter a word but the heat in the room began to subside, which was a great relief to all.

Alton rested his hand on top of the dragon's head saying, "Well done!"

At the same time a runner pushed his way into the room saluting at the Lord.

"Message from the village, Sir!" but then he saw the huge fluffy wolf-cat who occupied a big space in the centre of the room and at the same time realised that he had just run past a dragon!

"A dragon…!" he panted, "And what is that?"

"Calm yourself, man!" the Lord told him. "Report!"

"Word… word… from the village," he stuttered, "The… the rebellion has been overcome."

* * *

There was much to celebrate, and the ale ran freely. The people of the village laughed and danced, some very quiet and some with much gusto. They were so happy to be reunited with their families having been apart for so long.

Tan was relieved to find that his mother and sister were unharmed, and his brother too.

Autumn's parents too were thrilled to meet Neldon, along with Lindy, Ronan and the other Fair Folk who were also throwing themselves into the party spirit.

Whispers gradually circulated that it had been down to Alton, Tan and Autumn with their magical beasts who had helped to overcome the evil in the land. The five of them were feted and patted and even Blackberry received the kudos for his part in the affair. Talk was that Blackberry had teamed up with the blacksmith and used his hindquarters to kick enemy soldiers into the path of Autumn's dad where they were competently knocked on the head.

Shining Leaves revelled in the adoration of the villagers, Fair Folk and soldiers. Somehow the children of the village had got to know that his favourite snack was acorns and he was soon enjoying snapping in the air to catch the little goodies that were thrown to him.

Tan looked over at Autumn.

"Have you had enough of this?" he asked.

"I have, it's too much. If we could watch from afar without having to talk to so many people, that would be amazing."

"Let's go then!" he took her hand and they sidled off quietly. Autumn's mother looked over at her and blew her a kiss and smiled. There would be time for her family to get together when the festivities had died down.

"Hey! Wait for us!" a shout followed them as Otto came into view, Yulia beside him. She had been introduced to his two old friends earlier when he'd explained just how she had helped him. The four of them companionably went to join Blackberry in the stables where he was contentedly munching on hay in a net. He'd been allowed to roam at will, but it seemed he too, just wanted peace and quiet.

The three friends climbed up the hay bales which

were stored above the stable and settled themselves down exactly where they had used to sit when they were young, Yulia joining them as if she had always been part of the team.

A loud purr announced the arrival of Alpha, who padded through the doorway and sprang lightly across to nestle down next to Autumn, enjoying the gentle stroke down her back.

They had much to catch up on and for now any worry of what could happen in the future was pushed out of their minds. They were safe for the time being.

NOTE FROM THE AUTHOR

When I write a book, I never know exactly what is going to happen which means it's as much of a mystery to me as it is to you, the reader. I loved the way this story unfolded in my mind and do hope you find it as exciting as I did.

If you enjoyed it then please can you help me out by leaving a review on my Facebook or Instagram page or even Amazon, because as a self-published author it can be challenging finding new readers. It gives me such a boost when I hear from anyone who has enjoyed my stories and I do have such fun visiting schools and talking to children about my books, so if you can tell your friends and teachers about me, that would be fantastic!

Follow me so you can see when my next book is going to be released. It will be part two of this series.

Instagram: pamghowardauthor
Facebook: Pamghoward@pamghowardchildrensbooks
Website: www.pamghowardchildrensbooks.com

This book is printed on paper from sustainable sources managed under the Forest Stewardship Council (FSC) scheme.

It has been printed in the UK to reduce transportation miles and their impact upon the environment.

For every new title that Matador publishes, we plant a tree to offset CO_2, partnering with the More Trees scheme.

For more about how Matador offsets its environmental impact, see www.troubador.co.uk/about/